SHATTERED ICE

A SECRET MARRIAGE HOCKEY ROMANCE

POWER PLAYS & PUCKS
BOOK ONE

ISLA VAUGHN

ARROWSCOPE PRESS, LLC

(p) ISBN-13: 978-1-951919-73-3

(e) ISBN-13: 978-1-951919-72-6

Publisher: Arrowscope Press, LLC; www.arrowscopepress.com

Editing— Amanda K., Line Editor, Virge B., Proofreader, Red Adept Editing

Cover Illustration—Audrey Anhalt https://audreyanhalt.com

Cover Design—T.E. Black Designs; www.teblackdesigns.com

Interior Formatting & Design— Arrowscope Press, LLC; www.arrowscope-press.com

CHAPTER ONE

NYX

Every illusion I'd clung to had evaporated since my last call home. My hand shook as I smoothed down a few flyaway strands from my blond wig securely glued in place. Between that, the dress, and the contouring makeup and lash extensions, I could breathe a sigh of relief. They were my shield, a way to hide, an effective mask needed to endure whatever snide comments my stepsister, Trina, and her bitch crew would fling my way.

Across the street, a tall man with broad shoulders and dark hair stepped out of a sleek black SUV. I didn't mean to stare, but he looked like he belonged here, like the city bowed to him. His piercing blue gaze skimmed the crowded entrance, pausing for the briefest second when it met mine. Just a flicker. Barely a beat. But it made my breath catch, and sparks danced over my exposed skin, followed by the sensation that I'd been seen for the first time in months. The crowd swallowed him up as he entered the building, and I shook my head. Unreal. I must've imagined the intensity of our brief connection.

Vegas's neon lights and grandeur flashed and flickered above me as I stepped out of the cab, my stomach twisting into knots.

I tugged my wallet from my oversized purse and flipped it open with numb fingers. After the round-trip bus ticket and money for the cab, I had seventeen dollars. That was it. A crumpled ten, a five, and two singles. I shoved my wallet back into my bag like I could pretend this wasn't my life.

I shouldn't have come. Should've saved the cab fare and caught the last bus back home to California before it was too late. If I left now, I could still make it—if I were willing to sprint across the five blocks in heels and risk getting stranded at a grimy bus stop. But I already knew the answer. I had nowhere to go but back to my thirty-day-eviction-notice apartment, where the utilities had probably already been shut off. One night in a well-lit casino with an open bar wasn't the worst idea.

It didn't take long to find the roped-off room for the bachelorette party, sharing space with a crowd of oversized NHL players doing their rookie-initiation bonding night. Laughter spilled from the large private lounge as I approached, and Trina's shrill voice cut through the air like a knife.

"Margot!" she screamed at me, dragging out the last syllable like she was on stage instead of in a casino.

I cringed. Heads turned, and I resisted the urge to sink into the floor. Not my name but the alias I would answer to during Trina's party. Mine was ancient, meaning chaos, goddess of night, and feared by Zeus. Too bad I wasn't feared by anyone left in my family or the people in attendance tonight.

I adjusted the strap of the consignment-found, pale-pink embroidered halter dress and lifted the hem slightly. Delicate white feathers tickled my arms. I'd painstakingly adhered them to the waist, mimicking the nearly identical dress Margot Robbie wore to one of her Oscar red-carpet appearances. My spiky heels clicked against the polished floor, the unfamiliar shoulder-length blond wig snugly covering my long, dark waves. I looked nothing like myself.

Inside, the scene was pure extravagance, with glittering

decorations, designer dresses, and champagne flowing like water. The theme was undeniably Old Hollywood glamour. Feathers, diamonds, red lipstick, and gowns meant to walk the red carpet. The one rule Trina had insisted on? Blond bombshells only. Trina, of course, was Marilyn Monroe, her platinum hair perfectly styled, her red lips parted in a practiced sultry smile. The bridesmaids—aka the bitch crew—were different starlets—Cameron Diaz, Scarlett Johansson, Kate Upton—each glowing, radiant, and flawless. Then there was me, Margot Robbie.

As an attendant unhooked the red velvet rope so I could enter the gathering, Trina's smile faltered for a split second, hatred and envy eclipsing her brown eyes before returning to a brighter, faker gleam.

"I wasn't sure you would show. Thought you might be too busy… What are you doing these days?" Her head tipped back, her narrowed gaze peering beneath thick, long lash extensions. "Oh, that's right—nothing."

The laughter that followed sliced through me, and my cheeks burned as I forced a tight smile. "Nice to see you, too, sis."

She took a slow sip of her champagne before tilting her head, feigning innocence. Then she leaned close, her ruby lips inches from my ear so only I could hear. "Mom insisted you get an invite. It would have looked bad if she had completely shut out her dead husband's recently orphaned daughter. Can't have people talking, can we?"

I clenched my jaw, pain lancing me at the mention of my dad, who'd died a year and a half ago. My fingers tightened around my purse strap. The words shouldn't sting—they shouldn't be a surprise, but they burrowed deep anyway.

Her eyes flashed with a cunning edge. "If you play your cards right tonight, maybe you'll land someone who can pay your rent."

My jaw locked, heat crawling up my neck. I wouldn't give her the satisfaction. I wouldn't flinch or fold. I was here to survive the night, not get swept away in a fantasy. And yet... my gaze drifted, snagging on the guy from earlier at the far end of the bar. Tall, athletic, striking, he leaned back on his barstool like he owned the air around him. And when his head tilted and he grinned—directly at me—I felt something shift. Like maybe Trina's insult wasn't as far off the mark as I would like to admit.

The laughter that followed sliced through me, and my cheeks burned as I forced a tight smile. My teeth clenched as I ground out, "I'm not here to pick up a guy, Trina."

"Margot," she snapped, cutting me off. "We're doing things right. Address me as Marilyn."

I bit my tongue, nodding stiffly. Of course. Trina's world was one of carefully curated images and flawless—still-intact—illusions. There was no room for a sister she barely acknowledged outside necessary family functions.

I had a game to play, one that depended on my compliance or my witch of a stepmother wouldn't pay off one of the smaller college loans I'd carried since Dad died. She'd cut me off, hijacking my trust. No matter how hard I'd tried to continue at Brown University, I was forced to drop out from massive debt and lack of funds.

A circulating waiter handed me a glass of champagne, and I took a long gulp, grateful for the distraction and liquid courage. For reasons I couldn't explain, other than desperation, I would try to get along.

As I drained my first glass of bubbly, the music changed to something more current. A cry went out as several of Trina's group rushed to the dance floor, laughing and dragging Trina with them. I did a visual sweep of the room. Not everyone in the party was out there. A few groups of girls hovered along the edges. Some stood too close to the hulking hockey players for my taste. I shifted to the edge of the farthest group, who were deep in conversation, paying no attention to me as I lingered nearby.

The first drink went down too easy, the warmth spreading through my chest. When a waiter passed by, I set the empty on the tray and quickly grabbed another while watching the other bridesmaids twirl and pose, laughing too loudly, glowing under the glittering lights, and looking as if to gain the guys' attention. Trina had positioned herself in the center, moving like the world revolved around her—which it did.

"Shots!" The first of many shouts went up, and servers converged, passing them out.

I accepted the glowing green liquid and raised it high as Angela, Trina's bestie, toasted the bride. After touching the glass to my lower lip, I tossed it back, relishing the burn of whatever alcohol was in there. It was free—that was all that mattered.

Someone shouted for shots three more times, and the entire room obliged, even the guys—who I steered clear of, at least for the time being. Bass pulsed from the speakers, thumping in time with the beat of my heart, and I swayed to the music. For a moment, I felt like I belonged.

It didn't last.

Trina's voice cut through the alcohol haze like a blade as she stepped off the dance floor, a fine sheen of sweat coating her forehead. "Don't get too comfortable, Margot. This is the closest you'll ever come to being the star."

Laughter rippled from her minions' overly painted lips, Angela's the loudest. I wanted to punch Trina in her newly done nose. Nothing about her was real. I was shocked she hadn't chosen to go as Margot Robbie, decked out in an outfit from the Barbie movie. Even though, of the two of us, I was the one who looked almost exactly like the actress—something I'd down-played heavily with caked-on makeup and false eyelashes. I didn't want to look like myself, not here, not with the viper crew.

My stomach clenched, the warmth of the alcohol diminishing. I didn't know why I'd bothered. I shouldn't have agreed to come. *How did I think, even for a second, that I could slip into their world—the one I'd initially come from—for just one night?* If it weren't for the promise of a minuscule amount of debt relief, I wouldn't have.

Rather than lash out at Trina and her crew, I shut my mouth until she backed off. Playing with her prey was only so much fun if it didn't fight back. Chest tight, I pivoted and made my way to the bar near the rowdy hockey players, only glancing over them to ensure Trina's fiancé, Craig, wasn't close. With the coast clear, I bellied up to the bar, praying the drinks were free here too.

I gripped the edge of the smooth black counter as I waited for the bartender to notice me. Screw it. I flagged him down, ordered a cocktail that cost more than I could afford, and held my breath as I waited for him to tell me the cost. When he didn't, the knot inside my stomach eased, and my knees almost gave out at the gift of an open bar. I could part with a few of my meager dollars for a tip if I had to.

With my neatly poured drink in hand, I forced myself to sip the potent cranberry vodka, which was heavy on the vodka, knowing full well I would regret the hangover in the morning. But tonight, I craved the false bravado only alcohol could give. I needed one thing, just one, to help me feel like I belonged, even if it was only the drink in my hand.

The party roared on around me, but I barely paid attention as my gaze swept over the lounge's floor, landing on a group of giant hockey players gathered nearby in the VIP section. I knew very little about them from what Trina had grudgingly told me tonight. If the chatter was true, the newly drafted guys were being initiated into the team. Trina insisted on having her bachelorette party this weekend—here, to be exact—for one reason

—because Craig would be here. She wanted to keep an eye on him while pretending she wasn't.

I made the mistake of looking around at the partygoers again, and my gaze landed on Craig. He was laughing too loudly, flashing that fake, charming grin of his. He caught me looking, a glint flashing in his dark eyes.

My body went rigid. *Don't engage. Don't give him an opening.* I quickly averted my gaze, gripping my glass a little tighter. The way he watched me always made my skin crawl, and the last thing I needed was to get caught in his orbit.

The seconds passed in agonizing slowness as I waited for him to approach. My pulse beat a too-fast staccato beneath my skin, only easing when enough had time passed. I thought I was in the clear. But even with the reprieve from a confrontation with him, it couldn't fix the night from going bad to worse. The truth of my situation had me drowning. The eviction notice was plastered to my fridge with an ugly magnet. My student loans had piled up since Dad's death, and my stepmother's silence whenever I swallowed my pride and reached out for help was like an anchor dragging me under.

I lifted the glass to my lips and took a slow, burning sip. If nothing else, at least for a few minutes, I could pretend none of it existed.

CHAPTER TWO

MAV

My new teammates were rowdy, their energy buzzing as they celebrated the team's latest draft picks—myself and two other guys. Tonight was supposed to be a bonding experience, a hazing event disguised as team tradition before the preseason began—no coaches, no press—just the guys breaking in the rookies.

I'd been through many team nights before, but this was different. It was the NHL. The stakes were higher, the expectations heavier. My teammates ensured we knew what being a part of this world meant. Drinks kept coming. Women were everywhere, and bets were placed on everything. It was sensory overload.

"Davis." Kieran St. James, our captain, slapped me on the shoulder. "Not celebrating with the guys?" He gestured to the chaos behind us.

I smirked, lifting my glass. "This is me celebrating."

Kieran released a dry chuckle. "You're overthinking already, aren't you?"

I shrugged, not bothering to deny it.

His expression turned more thoughtful as he leaned against the bar, where I was nursing a whiskey.

"Look, Davis, I'm not here to kill the mood, but since we're outside team meetings and the arena, I figured now's as good a time as any to lay down some veteran wisdom."

I raised a brow. "Oh yeah? Should I take notes?"

"Don't blow smoke up my ass, kid," he shot back, grinning before his face turned serious again. "But yeah, maybe. Listen, you're stepping into a big role. It's a hell of an opportunity, and you deserve it. I've watched you at practice and even during your senior year at university. But the guy before you? Jennings? He had the same shot and similar talent. And now? He's done. Career torched, reputation in the gutter."

I frowned. "Yeah. I heard about that." Everyone had.

Steve Jennings had been the golden boy—until he wasn't. A scandal involving drugs, allegations of sexual assault, involvement with someone on the Titans' staff, and a locker room culture that had imploded because of his bad decisions and ego. The fallout was still fresh, and the team was under a microscope.

St. James exhaled, rolling his glass between his palms. It was the same one he'd had all night. "The league doesn't care how good you are if you become a liability. Jennings thought he was untouchable. Thought he could do whatever he wanted because of his talent, and the puck bunnies loved him. In his mind, rules didn't apply. And guess what? He's out of a contract, had to do some jail time, the team took a hit, and now every new guy, including you, has to prove we won't be the same damn mess we were last season."

I nodded slowly then turned, back against the bar, and scanned the room. "You think people expect me to screw up?"

"I think the league expects us to screw up." St. James gave me a pointed look. "And you? You're replacing the guy who set the team on fire from the inside out. You so much as sneeze the wrong way, and they'll be all over it. So keep your head on straight, yeah? No stupid scandals, no headlines, no distractions. We need you on the ice, not benched or fined before the season starts."

I tapped my fingers against my glass, the weight of his words settling in. "I'm not Jennings. Also, whose bright idea was it to hit up Vegas if we're trying to avoid a scandal?"

"I know you're not Jennings. It's just a friendly warning I'm issuing to all the rookies but especially you because of the forward position you're stepping into. As for the brilliant idea to come here, that would be Craig Ellis." He grinned. "At least no one is driving home, and hopefully, that mantra of *what happens in Vegas stays in Vegas* will work for us."

Before I could respond, Jensen Rhodes, our right winger, slid two shots toward us. "One for the rookie, one for the captain." He smirked, leaning against the bar.

Zane West, our defenseman, clapped me on the back, the shot held loosely between his fingers hovering close to my shoulder. "Take it easy. They're relentless, but you don't have to drown yourself."

I lifted my glass anyway, smirking as St. James grabbed his shot and clinked it against mine. I'd already had one too many but accepted it just the same.

St. James tipped his head toward me, amusement in his gaze. "Like I said, don't let the league own you." Then he tossed the shot back, pushed away from the bar, and squeezed my shoulder before disappearing into the crowd.

I watched as he walked off, blending seamlessly into the mix of players, flashing lights, and women.

No scandals. No distractions.

I took another sip of my whiskey, my gaze flicking toward the end of the bar where she was sitting—the girl in the figure-hugging pink dress with eyes that had already pulled me in like gravity. The bachelorette party theme was impossible to miss—

platinum blondes, satin gowns, red lips. But she stood out—Margot Robbie.

My teammates ordered another round of shots, and the girls in the bachelorette party were quick to join. A challenge was thrown, and suddenly, we were part of both celebrations. The chants of "shots, shots, shots" erupted around us—Craig's fiancée and her bridesmaids on one side, Kieran and the guys from the team on the other. There was no getting out of it. Glass after glass was pressed into my hands, the sharp burn of liquor turning into a pleasant sensation beneath the lights.

More drinks flowed, and the haze settled in somewhere between toasts and teasing. Margot's laughter came easier and looser from the antics on the dance floor, and my head felt light, making everything else—the stress, the pressure—blur into the background.

I slid onto the stool next to her. "Order you a drink, Margot?" I asked, my voice slurring slightly.

She turned her head slowly, arching a brow. "You know my name." Her voice was playful, but her eyes were at half-mast from the drinks. "But I don't know yours."

I smirked, swirling the whiskey in my glass. "Mav."

"Margot and Mav," she mused, testing how it sounded on her tongue. "Sounds like a disaster waiting to happen."

I laughed, feeling something easy and free click into place. "Vegas is built for bad decisions."

Her lips twitched, and she leaned toward me, her perfume mingling with the scent of whiskey. "Then let's not disappoint."

I tipped my chin toward the bartender. "Two shots of tequila."

She raised a brow but didn't argue. The bartender set them down a moment later, and we each reached for one.

"To terrible ideas," I said.

"To worse follow-through," she answered, and we clinked glasses.

The burn hit fast. She coughed through a laugh, wiping her mouth with the back of her hand.

I didn't give her time to think. "Come on." I stood, holding out my hand. "Dance floor's calling."

She stared at it for a second like she might say no—then slid off the stool and placed her fingers in mine. And when she followed me onto the floor, it felt a little less like a mistake.

CHAPTER THREE

NYX

The world came into focus slowly, one unpleasant sensation at a time—a pounding headache, the soft press of a pillow against my cheek, and, as I cracked open one of my heavy eyelids, the sun's rays spilling through an unfamiliar window. My lips were swollen, my throat dry, and my limbs ached with the slow, delicious soreness that only came from being touched everywhere—the kind of ache that lingered in the best possible way. I blinked, trying to clear the fog from my brain.

The sheets shifted against my skin, and my heart kicked into overdrive.

I'm not alone—and I'm naked. A sharp jolt of panic shot through me. My pulse pounded in my ears as I slowly turned my head.

A memory slid through the fog—his voice, low and amused as he asked if I always bit my lip when I was nervous. My lips tingled like they still remembered the graze of his thumb.

God, what did I do last night? And why does part of me want to do it again?

A large man lay sprawled on his back, his chest rising and

falling slowly, his dark hair mussed against the pillow. My gaze crawled over his gorgeous features from the jaw that could cut glass despite the five-o'clock shadow, firm lips, and slight crook in the bridge of his nose, to the spidery long lashes that should be illegal on any guy. The sheets barely covered his hips, and from what I could see of his well-defined body, he wasn't wearing anything either.

Mav. I remembered how piercing his blue eyes were and how, with one crooked grin, he'd made me want to make very bad decisions with him.

My stomach twisted, the pounding in my head intensifying as hazy flashes of the night before flickered through my mind—his lips on mine, his hands gripping my waist, lifting me, pressing me against the wall. The feeling of my legs wrapping around him and his breath hot against my skin. The rest was fuzzy.

My breath hitched. *What the hell did we do?* Or I supposed I should be wondering what we didn't do.

As slow as I could, I inched toward the edge of the mattress and carefully peeled the sheet off my body enough to slip out of bed. On shaky legs, I eased onto the floor, my heart in my throat and head ominously pounding while I kept watch over his sleeping form. I needed to get out of here, preferably before he woke. I didn't want to entertain an awkward conversation about whatever we'd done, not in my condition.

When I was sure I hadn't woken him, my gaze darted around for my things. I scrambled to gather the dress pooled near the bedroom door, my purse flung onto a coffee table in the suite's main room, and my panties hanging from a lamp next to the couch. Then I darted to the bathroom and carefully closed the door with a soft click.

After flicking on the light, I almost screamed. One of my eyelash extensions was stuck to my eyebrow. My lips were swollen, the lipstick smeared, and I wore most of last night's makeup and the blond wig that was messed up but still in place. At least no one on the hockey team, besides stupid Craig, knew who I was, let alone that I was Trina's stepsister.

The realization that my "mask" had remained in place gave me a small amount of the anonymity that I craved after doing only God knew what—or how many times—last night. Trina was always bitching about "hockey hookers" this or "puck bunnies" that—she would never let me live it down if she found out I shacked up with the California Titans' newest forward.

I peeled off the fake lashes, tossed them in the garbage, rummaged in my purse for makeup wipes, then got to work. It took a lot of wipes to attack the mess on my face. When I was done, I scrutinized myself in the mirror. Better, but I still looked like death warmed over.

Upon yanking my dress over my head, I shimmied into it. Then, heels dangling from my fingers, I eased the door open and tiptoed into the bedroom. A quick scan for anything left behind, and my gaze snagged on the crazy-hot man in the bed. An almost undeniable urge to strip off my dress and crawl back into his arms slammed into me. With a herculean effort, I tore my gaze away and turned to leave, when a crumpled piece of paper on the floor caught my attention. The edges were creased as if shoved hastily into a bag or pocket. My fingers trembled as I reached for the thick paper and smoothed it.

A marriage certificate. My stomach dropped. Maverick Davis. Nyx Lawson. *I used my real name.* The words blurred together as I stared at them, disbelief rendering me frozen. My name, his name. Official. Legal. A strangled noise escaped my throat before I slapped my hand over my mouth. *No, no, no.* I squeezed my eyes shut, willing the paper to say something else when I opened them again. It didn't.

Panic clawed up my throat. I glanced at Mav, still deep in sleep, unaware of the life-altering bombshell in my hands. *But if*

I don't remember getting married, and he drank just as much as I did... Maybe he won't remember either.

Screw it. I refused to stick around and have that conversation. With how my luck had been going, he could accuse me of entrapment. I couldn't take another hit. Instead of staying and asking him about what'd happened, I shoved the marriage license into my purse, burying it beneath my wallet and phone. If he didn't see it, maybe I could somehow find a way to get it annulled. Or perhaps I could just walk out of here, and this would disappear into the abyss of bad, drunken decisions.

My stepsister's shrill voice rang in my head, an ugly memory that lived on from last night. "You know, if you play your cards right tonight, maybe you'll land someone who can pay your rent."

I couldn't let her, or anyone, know about this. My stepsister would make it known that I'd set Mav up to solve my dire financial situation—and I hadn't. It was a nightmare. I had to get out of here.

I tiptoed toward the door, each step precarious. The cool metal of the doorknob in my hand felt like salvation, and with one last glance at the peacefully sleeping man, I twisted it, eased open the door just enough, and slipped out.

The hallway was eerily quiet compared to the chaos in my head. My heels dangled from my fingers as I padded barefoot toward the elevator, my heartbeat hammering against my ribs. *Please don't let me run into anyone from last night.*

It didn't take long for the elevator to arrive, fortunately empty. Once in, I stabbed the lobby button then slid my feet into my heels for as fast of a getaway as I could manage. The elevator dinged when it stopped, and the doors opened with a woosh, making me cringe as if a thousand horns had blared my entrance. I hurried out and wove through the thinned-out crowd of all-nighters and early-morning gamblers, keeping my eyes down. The air tasted stale, and my stomach rolled ominously.

Sunlight streamed through the tall glass windows, casting everything in unforgiving light. I had no idea if people stared or if I blended right in with my walk of shame—hair a mess and last night's dress wrinkled beyond repair. But I didn't care about that. I cared about forgetting. About pushing the whole night—and him—out of my mind before it could take root and grow into something I couldn't handle.

CHAPTER FOUR

MAV

The first thing I noticed when I woke was the quiet. I blinked at the ceiling, my head pounding with the after-effects of too much whiskey, too many shots, and too little sleep. My mouth was dry, my limbs heavy, but none of that mattered because the room felt empty in a way that sat wrong in my chest.

Extending my arm, I reached for her—the blond bombshell Margot Robbie look-alike whose features blurred in my mind ever so slightly—craving her softness pressed against me as it had been during the few hours we'd managed to sleep. But no one was there. The sheets were cool to the touch.

I turned my head, searching for any sign of her. The pillow beside me was indented, the sheets slightly rumpled, as if someone had just slipped away. A faint scent of something floral lingered in the air, clinging to the fabric, to my skin.

The night came back in hazy fragments—the burn of liquor, the press of her body against mine, her laughter, warm and unguarded. The way she'd looked at me like I was something more than a conquest or meal ticket. But the details blurred at the edges, slipping through my fingers like sand.

I should have been glad she was gone. I didn't need distractions, and from what I could remember of last night and the way she felt in my arms, I knew she would have been one hell of one.

Who was she?

I sat up with a groan, rubbing my hands over my face before raking them through my hair. The room was a mess. My clothes were strewn in a trail from the door—hers were suspiciously missing. An empty bottle of champagne and an overturned chair littered the floor. A glass sat tipped over on the nightstand, a few drops of amber liquid clinging to the inside. We'd celebrated hard. But she was gone.

I should've expected that. Vegas was built for temporary things—flashes of excitement that burned out by morning. But something about her not being here sat wrong in my gut, like I'd lost something before I even knew I'd had it.

I swung my legs over the side of the bed and planted my feet on the cool floor, trying to piece together the night. I squeezed my eyes shut, attempting to force details out of my scattered memories—the way her fingers had tangled in my hair, how she'd pressed against me like she already knew how well we would fit together. A rush of heat crawled up my spine at the ghost of the sensation, drowned out by frustration.

Why the hell can't I remember more?

My gaze swept the room again as I hoped for anything that might tell me something about the girl who'd disappeared before I could ask for more. But there was nothing. No number scribbled on a napkin, no forgotten piece of clothing, no trace of her other than the scent in the sheets and the lingering hum of something unfinished in my chest.

I exhaled sharply, scrubbing a hand over my jaw. It was just one night. One night in a city built on fleeting moments, on bad decisions that were meant to stay buried under neon lights and free-poured drinks. I should let it go. But as I stood, stretching the stiffness from my body, I couldn't shake the feeling that I'd let something vital slip through my fingers before I'd even had the chance to hold on.

CHAPTER FIVE

NYX

A week had passed since Vegas, but it felt like a lifetime ago. The glow of neon lights, the warmth of alcohol, and the freedom of being someone else had all faded, replaced with the cold, dull reality of my life.

The silence in my apartment was suffocating. My steps echoed against the hardwood floor, the only sound in the small, sparsely furnished space. I dropped my bag onto the kitchen counter and stared at the pile of unopened bills—student loans, utilities, rent. It was as if they were mocking me, a reminder of how far I'd fallen since my dad had passed away.

I reached for the eviction notice pinned to the fridge with a magnet and read the words for the hundredth time. Final Notice. Three weeks, and I would be out on the street. No amount of groveling would save me.

The guy from Vegas occupied my mind more than he should have. The one I'd kissed like he was air and I was suffocating. The guy who made me forget, even for a night, how close my life was to falling apart. Mav. I didn't even know if he remembered me, but sometimes, when the quiet got too loud, I thought of how he'd looked at me—like I wasn't a disaster waiting to happen. And that scared me more than eviction ever could.

I collapsed onto the couch, kicked off my shoes, and rubbed my temples. The dull throbbing in my head wasn't just from stress. It was sheer exhaustion. Another dead-end job interview. Another door shut in my face. I had been scouring job sites and pounding the pavement for days, searching for anything to pay the bills, but no one wanted to hire a college dropout with no relevant experience.

What the hell am I going to do? I fell back onto the couch, racking my brain for any answer to get me out of my mess. I couldn't go home—my stepmother said I wasn't welcome there. That particular asset, as well as everything else of Dad's, had become hers when he died. I'd already pawned my TV along with anything I could find to buy groceries, pay my phone bill— a necessity for potential job callbacks—and purchase bus fare to get to the few interviews I'd managed to score. Too bad they'd resulted in nothing.

The shrill sound of my phone ringing increased the tension headache building uncomfortably. I peeled one of my hands from my face and turned toward the screen, which flashed with a name I wasn't in the mood to see.

Why the hell is Trina calling? I let it ring, debating whether to ignore her. After a moment, panic set in about the agreement with my witch of a stepmother. I swiped to answer and pressed the phone to my ear.

"Nyx," my stepsister said, her voice syrupy sweet in a way that made me wary. "Did you make it home safely? You just disappeared. We were all so worried."

I snorted. "Worried? It took you a week to check in." Nope. She hadn't even wanted me there. This call was because she needed something.

A beat of silence followed before she sighed dramatically.

"Look, I'm busy planning a wedding. You disappearing without a word was rude, don't you think?"

I clenched my jaw. "I didn't disappear. I didn't stick around for the part where you pretended to care. I had to get back. Things to do."

"Whatever." Trina ignored the dig, breezing past it, like always. "I know things are... tough for you. But maybe if you tried harder, opportunities wouldn't be impossible."

"Right, because I just love struggling." I rolled my eyes. "Thought I'd make a game out of it."

She sighed again. "You're impossible."

"And you're only calling because you need something," I shot back. "Go ahead. Tell me. What do you want?"

Another pause before she exhaled sharply. "Fine. My bridal luncheon is this weekend. You're coming."

I nearly laughed. "Seriously?"

"Yes, seriously," she snapped. "People will ask about you if you're not there, and I don't need that kind of negativity right now."

"Right." Bitterness coated my words, no matter how hard I tried to hide it and my anger. "Because God forbid my dad's friends find out how you and your mother cut me off the second he died. What's in it for me, Trina?" Tears coated my eyes, but I refused to let them fall as I shoved myself into a sitting position on the couch.

I knew Cynthia, my dad's second wife, had hated me being underfoot when I took a year off from college to spend time with Dad while he fought cancer. He lost the battle, and the day after the funeral, that bitch kicked me to the curb.

I could've gone to a friend's house, but Cynthia had held my college tuition over my head. I went back to school, leaving California, and reenrolled for my junior year. Grief held me prisoner, and I isolated myself from friends until they stopped trying. A year later, after Brown had received minimal payments toward my Ivy League tuition, I was forced to leave. My debt was astronomical. Cynthia had reneged on her deal to make the payments, and I worried she would again with her latest demands, but it was a chance I had to take.

"Nyx!" Trina's voice pulled me from the past. "Are you listening?"

"I missed that last part. What was that?" I rubbed my forehead, wishing I'd never picked up the phone.

"I was saying… we didn't cut you off. You made your choices."

"Oh, you mean the choice to keep breathing after you both made it clear I wasn't part of your perfect little world anymore?" My grip tightened on the phone. "You don't give a damn about me, Trina. You don't want people whispering about how badly you've treated me. Or that your mother hijacked my trust." I didn't know how many times she'd convinced my dad to change the will and trust, but she'd accomplished what she'd hoped to—everything had been left to her in the end.

Trina made a frustrated sound but didn't deny it. "Just be there, wear something appropriate, and don't embarrass me."

I clenched my teeth. "You want me to go and not make a scene? Then you'll owe me." It was time I turned the tables for once if she didn't want me to mess with their carefully constructed social status that meant so damn much to them. "If you want me to show up so you and your mom can save face, then I need something from you—a job."

She was quiet for a second, and I could practically hear her weighing the cost of my attendance. "Fine. I might be able to pull some strings with Craig's team. They're always looking for assistants."

I hesitated, my mind tripping back to the suite in Vegas, leaving Mav before he woke, and what I'd found. It was a risk, but I didn't think he would recognize me. Then my gaze found and locked onto the eviction notice. Trina handled hiring for some roles in the league office. If she wanted, she could get me in the door.

"Anything would help," I admitted, my voice barely above a whisper. "And I need to know I have a job before this weekend."

"Don't get your hopes up," she replied breezily. "But I'll see what I can do."

She ended the call, leaving a hollow feeling in my chest. I hated asking her for anything. *But what choice did I have?* Plus, I finally had leverage, and I needed to be smart about it, even if Trina held it over my head.

Who am I kidding? Of course she would. She loved doing that. Still, if it meant a paycheck, I would deal with it.

CHAPTER SIX

MAV

The locker room buzzed with nervous energy that I remembered from my D1 college games, but this was my first exhibition game in the NHL. The air was thick with the smells of fresh gear and sweat and the faint tang of various competing deodorants and cologne. I'd been through training camp, worked my ass off in preseason drills, and even survived that initiation night in Vegas. But tonight was different—it was the real test.

I'd been playing hockey since I was five. The NHL was the endgame, and I would do my job to the best of my ability—my family was counting on me. I would not let them down.

I moved toward my locker, dropping my bag and focusing on the laces of my skates. The chatter around me was easygoing, but underneath it was something heavier—expectation. The guys knew me well enough by now. We'd been practicing together for weeks. They'd seen me on the ice and watched me handle the pressure, but games were different. I had to prove I deserved a starting position.

"Davis."

I glanced up as Kieran leaned against a row of lockers, arms crossed, watching me with that sharp, assessing look. Our captain wasn't a guy who wasted words. If he spoke, it meant something.

"Cap." I nodded, adjusting my pads.

"Coach tells me you're starting. You ready for this?" He pushed off the lockers.

All the rookies and second- and third-stringers would be playing. Veterans and starters played sparingly in exhibition games. It gave the rest of us a chance to prove ourselves. Plus, there was no reason to risk injuring our starting line in preseason.

I raised a shoulder. "Wouldn't be here if I weren't."

A few of the guys nearby chuckled, and the tension in the room lessened slightly. Kieran clapped me on the shoulder, his grip firm. "Good. Just don't let it get to your head. Stick to your game. Trust your instincts. You're here for a reason."

"Got it." I gave him a short nod, and St. James returned to his stall.

"Stick close to us, rookie," someone said to my left.

I turned toward Zane West, one of the team's defensemen.

He grinned as he leaned back on the bench. "You survive the first month without pissing anyone off, you just might make it."

"Good luck with that," another rookie, Beau Anderson, said. He had an easy confidence as he smirked. "I'm still waiting to stop feeling like fresh meat."

Nick Hayes, the team's starting goalie and one of the more seasoned guys, chuckled from down the line. "That's because you keep running your mouth, Anderson." He leaned back against the lockers like he had all the time in the world.

Anderson grinned. "Gotta keep things entertaining."

Hayes shook his head before shifting his focus to me. "Seriously, though, Davis, don't let it get to you. The first few weeks are rough, but you settle in fast. And if you ever need advice, find the guys who've been around awhile. We look out for our own."

I nodded, appreciating the words. "Thanks."

A sharp scoff cut through the moment. "If he even lasts that long."

I didn't need to turn to know who had said it. From the second I'd been drafted, Craig Ellis had made it clear that he saw me as a threat. He was an established forward but wasn't a star, not like he wanted to be. And the moment a younger, hungrier player had entered the picture, his insecurities had become impossible to ignore. He was like my cousin, who'd given the first-string quarterback and a few other starters at our college hell. I'd dealt with that shit enough not to let it bother me.

I met Ellis's gaze head-on. Sweat slicked his brow even before we'd taken to the ice, and for a guy trying to hold onto his spot, he wasn't hiding the strain well. His smirk was lazy, but his eyes were sharp, assessing. He was trying to get a rise out of me. I refused to give him the satisfaction.

"Guess we'll see," I said, keeping my voice even.

Ellis's smirk widened, like he was waiting for something else. When I didn't take the bait, he turned away, muttering something under his breath.

West nudged me. "Ignore him. He's just pissed the team's looking for fresh talent."

Hayes nodded. "Yeah, don't let Ellis get under your skin. His days of being top dog around here are numbered, and he knows it."

The words were meant to be reassuring but only solidified what I already suspected—I wasn't just here to play hockey. I was here to take someone's spot, and Craig Ellis knew it.

I exhaled slowly, shoving my bag into my locker. The pressure had been there from the start, and it only worsened with the shitstorm I sensed coming my way. After dropping onto the bench, I laced my skates as the locker room door opened, and one of the staff shoved his head inside.

"Davis, Coach wants a word."

I nodded, unlaced my skates, then shoved my feet back into my shoes while fully dressed in my gear. I pushed to a stand and followed him from the locker room. But the moment I stepped into the hallway, everything changed. I stopped short.

A woman stood there, poised but tense, her dark, wavy hair spilling past her shoulders, framing a face that looked familiar and yet entirely new. Her natural beauty and magnetism made it impossible to look away. My gaze crawled over her wide, upturned, striking blue-green eyes, radiant skin, and full, kissable lips. She was dressed in business casual, but something about the way she held herself made it seem like she was braced for impact.

Where have I seen her before? She looked familiar but not in a way I could immediately place. Her gaze locked on mine, her expression shifting from neutrality to wide-eyed panic in seconds.

"This is Nyx," the staff member said, oblivious to the tension crackling between us. "She's your new assistant and will handle your schedule, social media, and personal errands."

"Ah, I think there's been a mistake, but good to meet you, Nyx," I said, keeping my voice steady.

"You too," she murmured.

"Coach'll explain," the staff member said. "Nyx'll be waiting for you here after the game, and Coach is still expecting you."

My mind raced as I nodded at her then headed for Coach's office. I stepped into his office, the door clicking shut behind me. The room was small but efficient, with whiteboards covered in notes, game schedules, and player stats. Coach sat behind his desk, leaning back in his chair, his expression unreadable.

"Take a seat, Davis." He nodded toward the chair across from him.

I did as he asked, rolling my shoulders, trying to shake the tension from the exchange with Ellis and Nyx's sudden appearance.

Coach studied me for a long moment before speaking. "You've been handling yourself well through training camp. The guys respect you. You're showing the kind of discipline we want in a player."

"I appreciate that, Coach."

His expression didn't change. If anything, it sharpened. "But now comes the real test. Exhibition games are one thing. The regular season? That's a different beast." He leaned forward, resting his forearms on the desk. "You're stepping into a high-pressure role, Davis. You're replacing a guy who blew his shot and almost took the team down with him. We're still recovering from that mess and can't afford another scandal."

I straightened, my jaw tightening. "I'm not Jennings."

Coach exhaled through his nose. "No, you're not. But I've been doing this long enough to know the NHL can get to a guy. The pressure. The fame. The distractions." His gaze locked onto mine. "You've got the skill to be one of the best, but if your head isn't in the right place, talent means nothing."

"I can handle it," I said evenly.

He let that sit for a second before nodding. "Good. But handling the game is one thing. Handling everything off the ice? That's where a lot of players screw up. Don't screw it up like Jennings did. Keep your focus. No off-ice distractions—especially the kind that land you in the tabloids."

His warning and tone made my shoulders tense.

"That's why I pushed for you to have a personal assistant. Not just for the team's benefit but for yours."

I frowned slightly. "I can manage my schedule."

Coach's eyes narrowed like he knew I was about to be stubborn. "That right? Are you handling your dad's medical bills too? The insurance paperwork? The travel plans to see your folks when time allows? Or to have them come to a game?"

I flinched. I hadn't mentioned my dad's condition to the team, but it didn't surprise me that Coach knew. He made it his business to understand what was happening with his players, especially the rookies.

"I've got it under control," I muttered.

Coach shook his head. "Bullshit." He leaned back again, tapping a pen against his desk. "Look, I'm not saying you can't do it, Davis. I'm saying you shouldn't have to. You need to focus on hockey, not whether or not you paid your utility bill on time or booked a flight home for a few hours. Having a sick parent will mess with your head. Taking the day-to-day tasks off your plate will help so you can focus more where your attention is needed."

I exhaled slowly, running a hand through my hair. He wasn't wrong. Between practice, games, and checking in on my parents, I barely had time to breathe.

"I expect you to take advantage of the resources we're giving you," Coach said, his voice firm. "A personal assistant was assigned to you for a reason. Work with her."

Still, it bothered me to have someone's help. I'd always been self-sufficient, juggling and caring for whatever needed to be done. "I don't need—"

"Yes, you do," Coach cut in. "This isn't college, Davis. You're in the big leagues now. The team takes care of its own, but you have to be smart enough to accept help when it's given."

I pressed my lips together, jaw tight. I hated relying on someone else, but Coach wasn't giving me an option.

"This isn't a suggestion," he said, watching me closely. "It's already set up. I expect it to work out."

I exhaled through my nose, finally nodding. "Understood."

Coach studied me for another second then leaned back in

his chair. "Good." He gestured toward the door. "Now, get out there and focus on the game."

I pushed to my feet, my mind tangled with everything he'd said. As I stepped back into the hallway, my thoughts drifted to Nyx. She was supposed to make things easier. Minutes in, and she was making things a hell of a lot more complicated.

CHAPTER SEVEN

NYX

*O*f all the players in the league, how did I end up working for *Maverick Davis?*

When Alex, the Titans' staffing guy who'd introduced us, led me to a seat in the arena for the team's first exhibition game, I felt like I'd run an emotional marathon. I was completely wired when the team took to the ice. Mav was fast, more so than anyone on the opposing team. No wonder ESPN had named him the most anticipated rookie of the year and a guaranteed starter for the Titans.

I should have known my luck would run out when I'd convinced Trina to help me get a job where the guy I'd had a one-night stand with worked. My gut churned as I contemplated working with him. Never in a million years had I thought we would be paired together, which was why I'd gone through with my request—and to be honest, I was desperate. I needed money.

I'd blocked the possibility of ever seeing him again. *I mean, what are the odds?* He'd been out of sight, out of mind since our night together in Vegas. Add in that my TV was long gone, and I never watched ESPN. *Why would I?* But I didn't live under a rock, not when Trina's fiancé played for the Titans, which meant that I knew who was on the team.

Regardless, I'd entertained the idea that I wouldn't run into my one-night stand, which was ridiculous. Especially when Trina had stashed me in a room to fill out paperwork for the job and the sports show that was on kept talking about Mav. It should've been an omen.

When I saw him again, laughing with a teammate, that familiar edge of confidence in every movement, my chest tightened, flipped, and downright betrayed me. It wasn't just that he was gorgeous. It was that his presence gave the impression he looked at the world like it was his for the taking—and somehow that made me believe he would take me with him.

Does Trina know about me and Mav? I'm an idiot. Of course she must. That was why she'd helped me get this job without a blowup fight. That alone should've been a tip-off. I was just too desperate to realize she had ulterior motives, because there was no way she would have hooked me up with him out of the goodness of her heart.

Sitting in the arena, I'd racked my brain about it, but she rarely paid attention to me. Or she didn't unless she thought I was stealing attention from her—especially regarding her fiancé, Craig Ellis, current forward for the Titans. Trina could have Craig. I didn't care that he was a professional athlete, not that she believed me.

After the game ended, I returned to the hallway outside the locker room, and my situation hit me like a freight train. I was in a secret marriage that I needed to figure out how to get annulled without causing an even bigger disaster to befall me. I was stuck. I couldn't walk away from the job, not with my bills piling up and my eviction deadline looming. The thought of being out on the street with nowhere to go clamped like a vise around my stomach.

I can keep this professional. I had to. Besides, he didn't seem to recognize me. The sound of voices snapped me out of my inner debate as the door to the locker room opened and several hulking guys came out, Mav included.

"Davis, I need a word," someone yelled inside.

Mav turned toward the voice then back to me. "Give me a minute?"

I nodded quickly, hoping my face didn't betray the way my pulse sprinted. As he walked away, I greedily took in everything about him—the powerful way he moved, the easy confidence in his stride, how his broad shoulders filled out his team-issued hoodie. The scents of clean soap and faint cologne still lingered in his wake, teasing me and making my head spin.

Sure, I would keep things professional, but I was only human. The man was serious eye candy. I forced myself to stay rooted in place. My fingers curled into my palms to keep from fidgeting. My body wasn't cooperating, every cell in me too aware of him, my gaze locked on his impressive retreating form. I took a steadying breath, plastering on a neutral expression, willing myself to look like the professional I was supposed to be. I exhaled slowly in an attempt to relax and focus.

Just keep it together. Do the job.

Then I felt it—the prickle of being watched. I turned as Craig strolled toward me with the same smug, self-important swagger he always carried. A couple of players passed him without a word, giving him a wide berth. The gleam in his eyes made my skin crawl before he opened his mouth.

"So," he mused, stopping just close enough to make me tense, his sly smile and beady eyes way too insightful about where I'd been staring. "You're the new assistant?"

I crossed my arms. "I guess so."

Craig's smirk widened, his gaze bouncing from the door Mav had just gone through then back to me. "Trina didn't mention you had... history with Davis when I suggested you work with Mav instead of Dakota. Better to pair a rookie with a rookie."

I stiffened, cursing my unguarded expression when Mav's back had been turned, which Craig surely noticed. "We don't have history."

Fucking Trina. She and Craig had skin in the game of making me work with Mav, and I needed find out why before whatever bomb they'd planted could detonate.

"Right," he drawled, eyes flicking over me in a way that made my stomach churn. "Just a friendly warning, then—this place has a zero-tolerance policy on drama. Don't screw it up."

And there it was. I clenched my jaw, refusing to rise to the bait. But I should've known he would be in on taking any opportunity to sabotage me, just like my stepsister. Reminding me that I didn't belong was classic for Trina, and Craig was in on it. I had to watch my back so they couldn't get me fired. I needed this job too much to let anything stand in my way. This time, I wasn't rolling over. I'd done that enough since Dad died.

Craig leaned in slightly, his stale breath wafting over my face. "Listen up, rookie. You might've charmed your way in, but don't think that means you're safe."

I held my ground, staring him down. "I don't need to charm my way into anything, Craig."

His lips twitched like he wanted to say more, but then the door opened again. Mav stepped out, and Craig immediately straightened and moved a few inches away, adopting the fake air of professionalism he always used when someone was around.

I straightened my shoulders, pretending my heart wasn't hammering in my chest. Craig might have been playing games, but I had bigger concerns to worry about than his and Trina's verbal sabotage. Screw that. I was determined to figure out how to make myself invaluable as an assistant before it was too late.

The walk through the arena to the parking lot had been uncomfortably silent. I'd informed Mav I knew where he lived because the office had updated me with all the pertinent information and that I would meet him back at his place. From the stiff way he'd nodded, I could tell he was uncomfortable with the situation that appeared to have been coach mandated.

I met Mav inside the lobby. The building was a modern high-rise, unlike the dump I lived in. We rode the elevator to the fifth floor and stopped in front of his door. He pushed it open, stepping aside to let me in first. I hesitated before crossing the threshold, taking in the space.

It had an open floor plan, a terrace off the living room, and oversized windows that let in plenty of natural light during the day. From what I'd learned at the Titans' office, they owned several condos and rented them to their rookie players until they found a place of their own. It was what I expected—minimalist, expensive, and just messy enough to prove he lived there but didn't have the time or energy to deal with the details.

A duffel bag had been kicked against the couch. Unopened mail sat stacked haphazardly on the counter, and the scent of coffee and something woodsy that was undeniably him lingered in the air. I already knew he was leasing the condo for a year and that it was temporary while the season was in full swing, so he didn't need to look for a new place until after.

"So." He rubbed the back of his neck. "I, uh… I guess we should go over what you're supposed to do."

I turned to face him, setting down my bag. "I already have a rundown of what the role entails."

His brows rose slightly. "Yeah?"

I nodded. "Your schedule, appointments, travel, and general organization. That means I'll manage your calendar, handle social media, set up meetings, make sure you don't double-book yourself, and act as a point of contact between you and whoever needs to reach you—trainers, PR reps, management, and so on."

He folded his arms, nodding as he listened. "Okay. That all makes sense."

"There's also the logistics side," I continued. "Errands, grocery runs, dry cleaning, ensuring you have what you need when traveling. Some players opt for financial management assistance, but that's up to you. I've also signed an NDA, so you don't need to worry about information I handle leaking. Not that I would share anything about your personal life, but just so you're aware." My face heated. If he only knew the biggest secret I had on him.

Mav's expression flickered, and I could see the hesitation there. Panick surged through me, and I prayed the blond wig I'd worn in Vegas was enough to continue to hide my identity. Or maybe it was the money comment. I had no idea what his financial situation was like, but I knew that athletes often had more money moving in and out of their accounts than they had time to deal with, based on Trina's big mouth.

"I'll let you know about the finances," he said. "But the rest? Yeah, I could use the help."

I nodded, ignoring the way relief curled in my chest. "I'll put together a schedule for the week and email it to you by tomorrow morning."

His lips quirked slightly. "Efficient."

"That's the job," I said smoothly. I shifted, glancing toward the open space beyond the living room. "Where do you want me to work?"

He hesitated, rubbing a hand over his jaw. "I don't really… have a setup for this. But I have a spare room you can turn into an office. It's not much, but there's a desk and a decent chair."

"That works," I said quickly. A designated space meant I

wouldn't have to work from random coffee shops I couldn't afford or find excuses to linger at the arena longer than necessary. I would have to be there often when he was, but the less time there, the better. I would figure out ways to avoid him.

Mav went into the kitchen, opened a drawer, rummaged around, then held out a key for me. "Take this. If we're gonna do this right, you need access to everything."

I hesitated for only a second before taking it. "Thanks. I won't overstep."

He studied me for a moment then shrugged. "I trust you."

Something about how he said it made my stomach flip, but I pushed the feeling aside. This was strictly professional. Nothing more.

"All right." I gripped the key in my palm. "I'll get things organized and set up tomorrow."

Mav nodded, his gaze lingering on me for a beat longer than necessary before he turned back toward the kitchen. "Good. Let me know if you need anything."

I exhaled, steadying myself. This wasn't exactly what I had planned, but at least I had a place to work—a space that was mine, even if it wasn't home.

"By the way," I added, shifting gears, "I spoke with the team's nutritionist. I have guidelines on what you should eat, so if you're okay with it, I'll handle meal prep."

Mav raised a brow, looking half amused. "Yeah? That works."

"I'll make sure it's what you need." I hesitated before adding, "It'll be based on the guidelines, but let me know if you have any preferences."

His eyes flickered with something unreadable, but he didn't comment. Just nodded. "Sounds like a plan."

I swallowed back my relief. If I could make it to my first paycheck, I could cover my rent before they kicked me out. Every dollar would have to go toward it, which meant no extras

—not even food. The meal prep was supposed to be for him, but if I made just a little extra, enough that it wouldn't be noticeable, I would at least have something to eat.

I swallowed back my relief. I had three weeks before my eviction, and with a monthly paycheck coming soon, I had a plan.

CHAPTER EIGHT

NYX

Falling into a rhythm with Mav was easier than I expected. For the four days I'd been working with him, he'd constantly moved between exhibition games, practices, workouts, meetings, and media obligations. It kept him out of my way and me from reliving just how intimately I already knew him, in ways I had no business remembering. That left me to manage things without him hovering, being a trigger to my foggy memory of our night together, or second-guessing my every move.

I tackled whatever needed to be done—coordinating his schedule, making sure whatever he needed was packed properly before road trips. In addition, I handled his travel logistics alongside the team's coordinators and ensured any personal obligations for his parents didn't conflict with his demanding hockey schedule. I even took care of minor things like organizing deliveries and making sure his fridge had actual food instead of just protein bars and half-empty takeout containers.

I was wiping down the counter when Mav wandered in, shirtless, a towel slung around his neck from a late-night workout. His hair was damp at the edges, like he'd showered but hadn't bothered to dry it all the way.

"You don't have to do that." He nodded to the rag in my hand.

"You keep saying that," I replied without looking up, "but you also keep leaving crumb trails through the kitchen."

He leaned against the fridge, arms crossed, watching me in that unnervingly quiet way he had. "You organizing my life or just casing the place?"

I finally met his eyes. "Depends. Is your life this chaotic all the time?"

His lips curved into something wry, almost self-deprecating. "More than I like to admit."

The silence stretched. Not awkward. Heavy with something unspoken. The kind of quiet that curled into the corners of a room and settled there.

"You ever get tired?" I asked before I could stop myself. "Of being everyone's distraction, everyone's next headline, the guy who's always got it together?"

Mav didn't move for a second. Then he straightened, walked to the sink, and rinsed out his water bottle like I hadn't just asked something too personal. "All the time," he said finally, voice quiet. "But I don't get to fall apart. That's the deal, right?"

I wasn't sure if he meant being a pro athlete or being him.

My throat tightened as I folded the rag in my hand. "Yeah. I get that."

His eyes rose to mine again, unreadable but full of something I wasn't ready to name.

"Get some rest, Nyx," he said, his voice low. "You look like you're carrying too much."

"So do you," I whispered.

But he was already walking away.

When I'd gone through his mail and found his dad's hospital bills, I'd managed to set up digital access so he could keep up with them. I tried lying to myself that it was just about keeping things organized—handling what needed to be managed so he wouldn't fall behind. But that wasn't the full truth. Something had shifted for me. Not because of the bills themselves but because I saw the quiet way Mav had been holding everything together—on the ice, for his family, and even for me.

He hadn't stopped me when I found the bills. He'd trusted me enough to let me in, even accidentally. It made me want to be the person he could lean on, even if he didn't know how to ask.

God, when did that happen? When did I start caring that much? Maybe it was because I understood what it felt like to slowly watch a parent waste away, the pain of facing that eventual loss every time a new hospital bill arrived.

Even though we'd been working together for less than a week, I'd gotten pretty good at managing Mav's social media, posting small snippets from the home exhibition games or practices. We didn't cross paths often. I mainly updated him through text. Melanie, Trina's boss and the one who had trained me, had warned me that things would only get busier once the regular season kicked off. That was in six days.

For the most part, I stayed in my lane. When I needed to update him, I kept things professional—concise, direct. But sometimes, moments slipped through where he wasn't just my boss. Every clipped message and impersonal update felt like I was shoving bricks into a wall between us, even as cracks formed.

We were at the arena late, me finalizing Mav's schedule before the team's road trip after my latest discussion with Harper, the team's PR manager. I'd stayed longer than planned, fine-tuning a few things based on exhibition game coverage— scheduling interviews, handling media requests, and sorting out Mav's plans to visit a local children's hospital for cancer patients.

The arena halls were nearly empty when I finished making last-minute schedule changes. The silence gave me too much room to think about him, us, and how easy it would be to cross that thin line between assistant and something... *more*. The more time I spent with Mav, the more flashes of our night together hit me. The memories nearly took my breath away. They made meeting his eyes without blushing a challenge.

While I'd been busy adjusting his schedule, Mav had been handling post-practice media that wanted the scoop on the players' thoughts about the first game of the season. So, when he finally found me, I was still seated at the table in the conference room I liked to use, reviewing his updated itinerary. I barely noticed when he approached—not until he leaned over my shoulder, his presence pressing into my space.

I stiffened as his hand landed on the desk beside me, his heat at my back. Goose bumps rose along my neck, betraying me. His cologne—clean, woodsy, distracting—wrapped around me. I swallowed hard, my fingers tightening around the mouse.

"Why is the team meeting pushed up an hour before the flight?" His voice was a low rumble, his breath warm against my temple as he scanned the screen.

My pulse skipped at his proximity. *How can he unravel me with just his voice?* I had to force myself to focus. Not on him. Not on how close he was. *Concentrate. Numbers. Schedules. Anything but the heat crawling all over your skin.*

"Coach wanted you guys here an hour before leaving for the flight—specifically the newer players—and also to have extra time to review game footage before departure if you haven't already done so." I kept my tone neutral.

Mav released a dry chuckle, shaking his head. "If the guys haven't watched it by now, an extra hour isn't gonna fix that."

I lifted a shoulder. "I was told it's to keep the morning run-through from being rushed."

I turned to say something—anything—but our faces were

inches apart when I did. My heart fluttered. His eyes darkened, and for a heartbeat, it was as if he saw through my professional mask. His expression was unreadable, his jaw tight, his eyes warm in a way that made my breath hitch.

A slow beat passed, thick with something unspoken. Then, just as quickly, he straightened.

"Fine," he muttered, running a hand through his hair. "Just send me the finalized schedule."

I nodded, keeping my hands busy with the keyboard, pretending I hadn't just felt my stomach flip over itself. Mental distance. That was what I needed… but I was failing spectacularly at keeping it.

"You ready to head out?" Mav asked.

"Ah, not yet. In about fifteen minutes."

"I can wait," he said.

"No, it's good. Really. I need to stop by Harper's office before I go, and we'll probably walk out together."

I could almost see the shudder that racked Mav's body. All the hockey players feared the five-foot-five hell-on-heels publicist. It was the funniest thing I'd ever seen, but seriously, I wanted to be her someday. One look, and she could bend a hulking athlete into doing whatever publicity stunt she deemed necessary.

"I'll swing by your place later to finalize things."

Nick Hayes walked by the open doorway and paused, shooting us a lazy salute. "Careful in there, Davis. She's got that taskmaster scowl—deadlier than a slapshot."

I rolled my eyes and gave Mav's arm a gentle shove. He winked then left with Nick. Finally, I could breathe without his presence taking up so much space. But even with him gone, the air still felt thick with the heat of what had almost happened.

I should have gone home, but I was behind on one last thing —the gift Mav wanted to order for his parents. The recliner he'd found for his dad had suddenly gone on back order, and I'd spent the last hour hunting down an alternative that had better reviews and was also available for delivery late tomorrow afternoon. If I could make one thing easier for him, it would ease the weight I carried too.

When I found it, I double-checked that it was indeed in stock and would arrive when needed, then without talking to Harper, I raced out of the building and drove to Mav's.

He had asked me to handle that task personally, and I needed his approval on the final choice. That was the only reason I was still at his condo so late, pacing near the kitchen island with my laptop open when I heard the shower shut off.

I glanced toward the hallway just as he emerged from a cloud of steam, a towel slung over his shoulder, his dark hair still damp. He wore nothing but a pair of gray joggers that hung low on his narrow hips, clinging to his body in a way that made it impossible not to look.

I shouldn't have looked. But my brain betrayed me. No amount of pretending could erase the memory of Vegas and how he'd made me feel like I wasn't invisible for once. My breath hitched in remembrance of the press of his body, the rough scrape of his jaw against my neck, the way his hands had felt on my skin. I pressed my thighs together. A pulse of heat coiled low in my belly. *Damn it.* I quickly averted my gaze, forcing myself to focus on the open laptop. But I could still see him from my peripheral vision, his presence impossible to ignore.

"Something wrong?" His voice was rough, his tone casual as he ran a hand through his damp hair.

"No," I said too quickly, clearing my throat. "Just—your schedule is finalized and the coaching staff approved you flying to your parents' place after the game instead of home with the team. I also found a replacement for the recliner you wanted to order for your dad. It's better than the original one. It still has zero gravity but also a lift option in case he's too weak to get up on his own."

Mav stilled, his smirk fading. His gaze flicked to the laptop screen. "You found something better?"

His voice held surprise but something warmer, too, and I rubbed my chest at the sudden tightness there.

I clicked on the product details. "It's got the same comfort level but superior mobility features. Genuine leather, I checked. If I order tonight, it'll be delivered before your visit"—this weekend, and I planned to hang at his place, where the electricity bill had been paid, where I could read one of my favorite romances too. God, I missed reading—"white-glove service so your parents don't have to do a thing, or even rearrange what furniture they already have in the room it'll go in. The movers will do that for them—and I got it at a discount."

He exhaled, his fingers dragging through his damp hair. "You didn't have to do all that." His tone was rough, almost tender—like he wasn't sure what to do with the fact that I had.

"You asked me to handle it." I lifted a shoulder. "I handled it."

He studied me for a second, something unreadable flickering in his expression. Then he nodded. "Thanks, Nyx." His voice was quieter now. "That means a lot."

I looked away, closing my laptop. "I'll, uh… finish up the order now. I'll also check you in for your flight and send everything to your email, including texting a screenshot of the boarding pass in case the airport has any Wi-Fi issues."

"Thank you." He didn't move right away. He just watched me for a second longer before finally turning to grab water from the fridge.

I took that as my cue. Grabbing my bag, I moved toward the door. Leaving felt like the smart choice. *So why does it also feel like running?*

He didn't stop me, and I was eternally grateful. I feared I would climb him like a tree if he'd even put a hand on my arm.

When he was too close and smelled incredible, he was impossible to resist. It made the night we'd shared refuse to stay in the mental box I'd tried to lock it in. The car ride home passed in a blur, my body recovering from the magnetism I felt around Mav. Preservation won out, which meant I was that much closer to escaping a life of homelessness.

I tried to put the undeniable chemistry between us—which might have existed on only one side, mine—behind me. But back home, as I lay in bed later, staring at the ceiling, my body still humming from a memory I shouldn't hold on to, I knew it wouldn't be that easy. Staying invisible but still indispensable was a lot harder when the one person I needed to avoid was impossible to ignore.

CHAPTER NINE

MAV

I'd thought I was prepared. But no amount of bracing could soften the blow of watching someone I love slipping away inch by inch. The whole flight home, I'd told myself it wouldn't be as bad as I feared, that my dad would still be my dad, that he would crack a joke or at least pretend for my mom's sake. But the man I saw sitting in that recliner, frail and exhausted, was barely a shadow of the father I'd known. The chemo had drained him, left him gaunt and weak, his skin pale, his hands trembling even when he tried to wave me over with a tired smile.

I sat with him for hours, talking about hockey, my first weeks with the team, and anything but what mattered because neither of us wanted to say it—that he was sick, that it was getting worse.

My mom held herself together until I was leaving, then she clung to me at the door, whispering, "I'm so proud of you," like she was afraid she wouldn't get another chance to say it. And that terrified me.

By the time I landed back in California, I was raw, worn down. I just needed silence, a second to breathe. But what I found when I opened the door wasn't relief. It was temptation, waiting for me in my living room.

Nyx was stretched out on the couch. She looked like she belonged there, dammit. Like the space had shaped itself around her as she watched TV, curled into the cushions, a bowl of apple slices on her lap. Her tiny shorts rode high up her thighs, and the fitted gray T-shirt hugged her curves, making my jaw clench. I knew I should look away, keep walking, pretend I hadn't just let my gaze linger a little too long on the smooth lines of her legs.

It was dangerous territory, but I'd already crossed the lines too many times in my mind to stop. Over the last week, pretending I hadn't noticed had been increasingly harder. It was hell having her so close but untouchable. And worse, there was something about her that I couldn't shake. My chest tightened whenever she was near. I'd studied her face a hundred times. The familiarity twisted my gut—like déjà vu and longing colliding at full speed. I swore I knew her, somehow. But she always sidestepped personal questions, changed the subject, and made it clear she was here to do a job.

But the way she's dressed right now? This wasn't her on the job. It was the first time I'd seen her casual, effortless, and too damn sexy for her own good. In my condo, on my couch, and off the clock.

She'd booked me on a later flight. I'd changed it, left an hour earlier. *Had she planned on escaping before I got home?* All signs pointed to yes. Because this—this was different. And I wanted more of it.

Nyx jumped when she saw me and scrambled to her feet as I dropped my bag by the front door. "I'm sorry," she blurted, clutching the bowl. "I must've lost track of time. I didn't think you'd be back so early. I was just—"

I cut her off by plucking an apple slice from her bowl then waved her back toward the couch. I liked how real she looked.

Not the reserved assistant but relaxed, at ease. She never needed makeup and rarely wore it, and that appealed to me a hell of a lot.

I watched her, trying not to get caught up in the way her lips moved or how at home she looked. Not a lot of the silence in my life felt good. *But this?* This quiet moment with her settled under my ribs.

"Sit." *Stay, so I don't have to wonder what it would feel like to have you here, really here.* I liked that she'd decided to make herself at home in my place while I was gone.

"I was just finishing up a few things and hadn't dressed for work because—"

"It's fine." I waved away her worry.

Her lips parted like she wanted to argue, but after a beat, she hesitated then slowly sat back down. I dropped onto the opposite end of the couch, stretched out, and let my head fall back against the cushions as I took a bite of the apple.

"How was your trip?" Her voice was softer. She didn't fill the silence with empty platitudes. She just… asked, like she actually cared.

I exhaled, staring up at the ceiling. "Bad." The single word tasted bitter in my mouth, raw and exposed.

She didn't push or throw out an automatic, empty "I'm sorry." Instead, she just waited. So I talked. I told her about my dad, about how thin and weak he looked and how it was getting harder to pretend everything was fine. About my mom, the way she tried to hold it together, and how it shattered something in me every time she looked at me like my visit home could fix any of it.

"I called Skye, my friend and former next-door neighbor. She gets it. She knows my dad well," I admitted, giving her some context while dragging a hand over my face. "I figured I just needed to talk it out, but she was busy with her family, and I wasn't up to crash their night. I talked to her daughter, Lily, for a bit, but after that, I didn't have it in me to lay all this on her, no matter how hard she pushed."

Nyx shifted beside me, pulling her knees up to her chest. "So you came home instead of going to see her?"

I turned my head toward her, studying the way the light from the TV flickered against her face. "Yeah."

"And you wanted to talk some more."

I let out a low, humorless laugh. "Guess so."

She nodded once then simply said, "Then talk."

No judgment. No pressure. Just quiet understanding. And it undid me. The words spilled out, the weight of them pressing against my chest as I finally let myself admit how damn hard it was—how much it scared me. She listened, her gaze steady, understanding, her presence grounding in a way I hadn't expected.

She was quiet for a moment after I finished, her fingers fidgeting with the hem of her shorts. Then, softly, she said, "I know what that helplessness feels like."

Her words didn't just hit me—they leveled me. "You do?"

She nodded, exhaling slowly. "My dad passed away a little over a year ago. It was... the hardest thing I've ever been through." She swallowed, her throat bobbing. "Watching someone you love fade like that, knowing you can't do anything to stop it? It changes you. You don't go back to the person you were before." Her gaze dropped to her hands, like the weight of her past still lingered there.

Something in my chest tightened. "I'm sorry."

She gave me a small, sad smile. "Me too." She shook her head. "After he was gone, I used to think if I just stayed busy, kept moving, I wouldn't have to deal with it. That if I ignored it long enough, the grief wouldn't catch up with me." She let out a soft, humorless laugh. "Spoiler alert—that doesn't work."

I studied her, taking in the way she stared at the coffee table like she wasn't seeing it.

"What does?" My voice came out rougher than I'd intended, like I already knew the answer but needed to hear her say it anyway.

She looked up then, meeting my gaze. "Letting yourself feel it. Permitting yourself to break down when you need to." Her voice was gentle but firm. "And being there with him as much as possible. Because, one day, you might not get that option again."

I sucked in a breath, the truth of her words hitting me hard. She wasn't wrong. Every time I walked out my parents' door, I worried it would be the last time I saw my dad alive. I didn't want to say it out loud, but the thought had been gnawing at the back of my mind since I'd left home.

She hesitated then shifted toward me. "Mav, if I can do anything to ensure you get home as often as you need to… just say the word."

Her words felt like a lifeline, as if I wasn't drowning alone. "Nyx—"

She shook her head. "I mean it. I'll make sure your schedule works around visits as much as possible. You shouldn't have to choose between hockey and family."

I let out a slow breath, the tension in my shoulders easing slightly. "That… would mean a lot."

She nodded, offering a small smile. "I've got you."

God help me, I wanted to believe her. I wanted to believe in her.

She placed her empty bowl on the coffee table and grabbed the remote. Without thinking, I stretched my arm along the back of the couch. When she leaned back, her bare shoulders brushed against my skin. A spark shot through me, fierce and unwelcome. But I didn't pull away.

Her breath hitched, she fumbled the remote, and I felt the shift. The way her pulse fluttered at the base of her throat, how her grip tightened. She was hyperaware of me, just like I was of her.

I should have removed my arm, given her space. But I didn't. Instead, I reached for the remote and took it from her hand. Our fingers brushed. The touch was brief, but neither of us moved away immediately.

Her hand trembled. "Sorry."

I blinked, tearing my gaze from her mouth. "No worries." The lie felt heavy. Something charged passed between us. It would've been so easy to pull her in and kiss her until all the noise in my head stopped. But I didn't.

She nodded, holding my gaze a second too long before looking away. My fingers curled against the couch, and I resisted the urge to reach for her. The air between us stretched, tense and thick with need.

Then she shifted, drawing away from me and standing. "I should go."

I forced myself to stay still, not to pull her into my arms, not to ask her to stay. "Okay." The word felt wrong in my mouth, but I let her leave to put the dish in the dishwasher and walk away.

She grabbed her bag and paused briefly by the door before slipping into the night. And with her went the last thread of my self-control.

I wasn't the only one feeling this. I needed to get it together. I'd probably already broken half a dozen HR rules—or was close to it. *And the worst part?* I needed her. She was my assistant, not some girl I could afford to want.

But the truth hit me later that night, alone in my condo. Something was unraveling inside me. And I wasn't sure I wanted to stop it.

CHAPTER TEN

NYX

I had barely slept. Every time I closed my eyes, I saw how Mav had looked at me last night—like I was a puzzle missing its corner piece. The sharp focus in his gaze, the way his brow furrowed like he almost recognized me but couldn't place from where, and it terrified me how much I wanted him to figure it out.

I had been so careful the past few weeks—maintaining my distance, keeping things professional, making sure he never had a reason to look too closely at me—but last night had unraveled that careful distance. Every barrier I'd built between us felt thinner, like tissue paper that had been soaked through. Talking to him, listening to him confide in me about his dad, had made things seem too easy, like I belonged there—which was dangerous.

I moved through my morning routine like always—quietly, efficiently, staying out of his way. He was already up and gone for practice by the time I emerged from my designated office in his condo. I was relieved. I needed space to remind myself why I was there, space to remember the stakes and pretend the skip in my heart wasn't real.

I wasn't his friend. I was his assistant. And if he ever realized who I was—who I had been to him in Vegas—it would all come crashing down.

By the time I arrived at the practice facility, tension coiled between my shoulder blades like a tightrope ready to snap. Things were so complicated. Mav wasn't just my boss. He was also my husband, even if he didn't know it. *But the way his fingers brushed mine last night?* It seemed intentional. I shook my head. I was reading into things. He didn't recognize me. He was tired, overworked, and worried sick about his parents. I needed to get over myself. As for the marriage, real or not, I would eventually need to figure out how to annul it. I had the document shoved in my work bag to deal with when I had time. For now, out of sight, out of mind was the way I was handling it.

I kept my head down, but I couldn't shake the awareness between us. Like a magnetic pull beneath my skin, always humming and present. It was in the way his gaze caught on mine, lingering a second too long. The way my stomach flipped when his shoulder barely grazed mine in passing. I couldn't ignore it.

I'd planned to hang around the stadium during practice, knocking out a few tasks while the guys were on the ice. As I walked through the halls, Mav rounded a corner ahead. The second he saw me, he grinned. I hated how easily he could unsettle me without even trying. I forced my expression into something neutral, professional—anything but the way I really felt.

As we closed the distance, he hesitated then held out a cup of coffee. "Figured you could use it."

His fingers brushed mine when he handed it over—warm, calloused, a blink-and-you-miss-it touch that lingered longer than it should've. He didn't look at me when he set it in my hands, but there was a calmness in him, like he'd made a decision and was already at peace with it. No teasing, no smug smirk. Just… caring. The kind that chipped away at my walls without asking permission.

I blinked at the cup I suddenly clasped. My fingers wrapped around it too tightly, as if the warmth could ground me, but it only made my pulse race faster. In the short time I'd known Mav, I'd never seen him do something like that. Before I could say anything, he was walking away. That was when I knew—I was in too deep.

I turned, expecting to see his back as he disappeared around the corner—but he'd turned back to face me. Mav stood a few feet away, his head tilted slightly like he was trying to read my mind. The noise of the hallway faded beneath the weight of his stare.

"You okay?" he asked, his voice low. Not flirty. Not sarcastic. Just… genuine.

My heart stuttered. It shouldn't have mattered. I was used to pretending. Used to being fine, no matter what. But for a split second, I wanted to tell him no. That I wasn't.

"Yeah," I managed. "Just tired."

He nodded then, just like before, he turned and walked away —leaving me standing there, clutching the coffee like it was the only solid thing in my world.

I shoved the thought aside, turning my focus back to work. I was here to do my job, not to get distracted. Still, I couldn't ignore how some of the guys milling about gave me lingering glances. Being a female assistant in a testosterone-heavy environment was already hard enough—I didn't need to provide them with more reasons to assume things about me.

About to head into the arena, I rifled through my bag with one hand, realizing I had forgotten to bring a bottle of water. They had a fridge in the break room, and I went to grab one from there. I planned to sit in the arena during practice and finish everything I needed to do, uninterrupted. As I reentered the hall, I fell into step behind some players heading toward the locker room before practice. Their voices were loud, making it impossible not to overhear them. Before I could turn away, I heard my name and dropped back to make my presence less obvious.

"Davis has it made. First-year guy, and he already landed a hot assistant," said one of the hockey players I couldn't quite see. "My first year, I got saddled with Rick, not with a hottie like Nyx."

I froze in mid-step, my breath catching. I knew who the guys were. I'd made a point of memorizing every player's face, their names, and their significance. Pretending not to recognize the voice wouldn't make the words any less humiliating.

"Yeah," defenseman Ethan Mercer added, his tone laced with amusement. "Wouldn't mind having someone like her handling my schedule." He smirked, his too-confident voice curling around the words like he thought he was clever.

Laughter rumbled between them, low and knowing, but Craig's voice sent ice down my spine.

"Please," Craig drawled, dragging out the word like he was humoring a roomful of idiots. "She's not here for the job. Girls like that? They show up when the money's fresh and the press is watching. Convenient timing, don't you think?" He smiled, slowly and smugly. "Hell, if Trina didn't have me on a leash, I might've recruited her myself. But lucky for me, my assistant knows how to keep things… quiet."

Logan Reeves chuckled a beat too late at Craig's joke, like he didn't quite get it but wanted to stay in the fold.

Heat flooded my face. Craig was such a jackass. I curled my fingers into fists, nails digging into my palms, forcing myself to breathe and remain calm. It would only make things worse if I walked out there and let them see that they'd gotten to me.

"You think she's playing the long game?" Tim Shaw's voice dripped with mock curiosity as he leaned forward a little too eagerly. "Or just genially doing what the job entails?"

"Hell, look at her. Gorgeous or not, she's running herself ragged. Maybe she's not just exhausted but using something to keep up." Mock sympathy dripped from Craig's every word. "Wouldn't be the first time someone rode that wave straight to scandal."

Laughter. More jokes. I wanted the floor to swallow me whole. The only good thing about this was no one had spotted me yet. Zane West and Nick Hayes entered the hallway right before the entrance to the locker room, where the other guys had caught up. None of them looked pleased, which gave me hope they wouldn't let what Craig said go unchecked.

"Maybe shut the hell up, Ellis." Zane's voice cut in, sharp and irritated. "Not everyone's as miserable as you." He crossed his arms, muscles tight under his hoodie, like he was two seconds from throwing a punch.

A brief pause followed. The tension shifted.

"Relax, West," Logan Reeves muttered. "It's just locker-room talk."

"Nah," Nick said coolly. "It's just bullshit. And you're damn lucky Harper hasn't caught any of the crap you're sprouting. She'd have your asses in another four-hour mandatory sexual harassment class." He didn't raise his voice, and he didn't need to. His words cut sharper than a knife.

I didn't wait to hear more. Shame prickled hot beneath my skin, chasing me down the hallway like a shadow I couldn't outrun. As soon as the hall was clear, I turned on my heel and walked away, my pulse hammering.

I had been prepared for Trina to make my life hell. I hadn't thought Craig would take such a public interest, but I should have. He had never liked me, and now he had an audience. *The worst part?* Though Zane and Nick had spoken up, I still felt alone.

My stomach twisted in knots. The arena walls suddenly felt too close, the air too thick. A wave of nausea rolled through me so suddenly, I had to stop, pressing a hand against my abdomen.

Stress. It was just stress. But deep down, I wasn't sure that was all anymore.

I inhaled slowly, forcing myself to breathe through it to steady my nerves. Because I couldn't afford to fall apart. Somehow, I managed to walk past the closed locker-room doors, down the hall, and into the stands, where practice would be happening on the ice shortly. I took slow, measured sips of water.

The chill of the arena frosted the air. Practice hadn't officially started yet. Skates scraped against the ice below. I didn't know who was on the ice, and I didn't care.

I kept my head down, eyes locked on my laptop screen, but my mind was elsewhere. Craig's words still echoed in my head. No matter how many times I reminded myself not to care, the sting burrowed deeper. The way the other guys had laughed, how no one had defended me before Zane and Nick stepped in. It shouldn't have mattered—I wasn't here to make friends. But that didn't stop the impact.

I forced myself to focus, scrolling through Mav's upcoming itinerary—PR requests, travel logistics, and media interviews—anything to keep my brain busy.

"Please tell me you're not buried in emails and spreadsheets at a time like this."

I glanced up just as Vivi, wife of Jenson Rhodes, dropped into the seat beside me, her dark curls bouncing and bracelets jingling as she set down a cup of iced coffee with a dramatic sigh. Selene St. James, wife to the Titans' captain, slid in across from me, resting her chin in her hand with an amused smirk.

"She's working," Selene teased, nudging Vivi. "Look at her. Locked in."

Vivi snorted then tapped her nails against the plexiglass

separating us from the rink. "Even while sitting in front of the jock aquarium. Hard to believe."

I blinked at them, caught off guard but trying not to laugh at Vivi's statement. Instead, I addressed Selene's. "Uh, yeah… kind of comes with the job."

Vivi rolled her eyes. "Okay, well, I come with my job, which means mandatory gossip breaks." She leaned in conspiratorially. "I was just about to tell Selene—Jenson tried to surprise me with dinner last night, except he forgot that he can't cook. Like at all."

Selene burst out laughing. "Wait—what did he make?" She tapped her perfectly manicured nails against the armrest as if she already knew the ending to the story I hadn't caught up to.

Their easy friendship felt like sunlight on my skin, a momentary shield against the storm inside me.

"Burnt steak and something that was supposed to be mashed potatoes but had the consistency of glue." Vivi groaned, covering her face. "I swear, I love that man, but he should not be allowed near a stove."

A surprised laugh escaped me before I could stop it. "That bad?"

"Worse." Vivi nodded solemnly. "But at least he tries. Unlike some men I could name." She tilted her head meaningfully toward the ice, where a few guys were skating. I casually glanced around, but Mav wasn't out yet. Most of them weren't.

Selene smirked. "Speaking of men…" She propped her chin on her hand again, watching one of the players skate past. "You know Mav sneaks glances at you, right?"

I stiffened. "What?"

She grinned. "Oh, don't act surprised. It's subtle, but it's there. The second he thinks no one's watching? Boom. Eyes on you."

Vivi nodded. "It's kind of adorable. Big, tough hockey player preoccupied with his assistant working in the stands."

Selene cackled, slapping Vivi on the shoulder. "Kind of like how you and your husband met. Didn't he get slammed into the plexiglass right where you sat?"

The mention of "husband" twisted something sharp in my chest. Too close to a truth no one knew.

"Love at first sight?" Vivi grinned. "I wonder if that's what's happening with you and Mav." Her bright-blue eyes locked on mine.

"I—he does not." My face felt hot. "He's just..." A complication I couldn't afford. A temptation I couldn't resist.

Selene arched a brow. "Just what?"

I fumbled for a response, but nothing came out. They exchanged a knowing look, and I exhaled sharply, shaking my head. "You guys are ridiculous."

"Uh-huh." Vivi leaned back, sipping her coffee. "Deny it all you want, but we see things."

I rolled my eyes but couldn't stop the small smile tugging at my lips. It was a welcome change from the sneers and whispers. Warmth bloomed in my chest, unfamiliar and almost too much to handle.

Before I could argue further, a shiver danced along my spine, like I was being watched. I turned instinctively and found him. Mav. He skated across the ice, his gaze locking on mine for several seconds.

The teasing silence from Vivi and Selene was deafening.

I swallowed. Mav didn't come closer. More players poured onto the ice, and practice got underway, but my face felt heated. The second I caught Selene's eye, both women smirked.

"Uh-huh. Not looking at you, right?" Selene laughed.

I groaned, but deep down, the warmth in my chest spread. Against my better judgment, I let it. Just for a moment, I let myself feel it. Maybe they were ridiculous, or maybe they saw something I was too afraid to admit.

CHAPTER ELEVEN

MAV

The locker room had carried a different energy today—quieter, more focused—as the usual pre-practice chatter hummed in the background, the occasional clatter of skates against the rubber flooring or the snap of a stick against a locker filling the space. I was halfway through lacing up when I caught Ellis's voice carrying over the noise, too loud, too smug.

"Man, Vegas was a hell of a time." His tone dripped with amusement. "You know, some girls go there for a good time, but others? They're playing the long game."

My hands stilled on my laces. My chest tightened, muscles coiling like I was bracing for a hit. Ellis leaned against the locker next to mine, arms crossed, eyes filled with something calculated.

"Keep an eye on your new assistant," he said, voice just low enough to sound like a warning. "She's got a reputation."

The words landed like a cheap shot to the ribs. Unwelcome, unearned. I glanced up, meeting his gaze. "That right?" My tone was flat, but tension curled in my gut.

Ellis shrugged. "Just saying, Davis. You're the new kid;

maybe you don't know how things work yet. Girls like her? They latch on. You think she took that job for the paycheck?"

I exhaled slowly, forcing myself to stay seated. "You've got a real talent for talking shit, Ellis. Maybe focus on your game before you drag someone else's name through the mud."

"Hey, she's trouble, but do what you want." He smirked. "Just don't say no one warned you when you end up following in Jennings's footsteps."

I clenched my jaw, forcing myself to ignore him. My fingers tightened around my stick as I stood, but St. James's voice cut through the tension before I could think of a response.

"Enough, Ellis." The team captain's tone was sharp, final. "Get on the ice."

Ellis held my gaze for a second longer before scoffing and skating off, his little entourage—Logan Reeves, Ethan Mercer, and Tim Shaw—following closely. The trio flanked Ellis like backup dancers, laughing too loud and waiting for cues to obey.

Our starting goalie, Nick Hayes, leaned against his stall, watching the exchange. "You good?" he asked, his tone casual but his eyes sharp.

"Yeah," I muttered. "Nothing I can't handle."

Hayes hadn't looked convinced, but he'd let it drop.

Some tension eased from my shoulders when my skates hit the ice. The cool air filled my lungs, steadying the burn in my chest. This was what mattered—drills, competition, the game itself. Nothing Ellis said could change that.

My gaze instinctively searched the stands until I found Nyx. She laughed softly with Rhodes's and St. James's wives, her expression open in a way that always caught me off guard. She must've felt me watching, because she turned—eyes locking on mine like she'd been waiting for it. A flush crept up her neck, and I couldn't help wonder what they'd been talking about. *Or maybe she was just thinking of me?*

"All right, rook, let's see what you've got," Rhodes called out, skating beside me. "We're running zone-entry drills. You ready?"

I nodded. "Yeah. Let's go."

Rhodes nodded before pushing off, leading me into the drill. We moved through transitions, one-timers, speed bursts— everything I'd spent years refining but now under the scrutiny of an NHL team. St. James joined in, running plays with me, testing my reaction speed and chemistry with the line. I focused and let my instincts take over.

But every time I glanced up, I caught Ellis watching. His gaze was a thorn beneath my skin, a constant irritation of a threat. His agenda wasn't just competition. It was personal.

Rhodes smacked his stick against the boards. "C'mon, Davis —don't go soft on me now."

"Davis, pick it up!" Coach barked from the bench. "You're holding back."

Anger churned beneath my ribs, hot and restless. I would give them something to talk about. Gritting my teeth, I pushed harder, cutting through the defense, my stick snapping against the ice as I sent a clean shot toward the net. The puck flew past Hayes and hit the top shelf.

"Damn," Hayes muttered, shaking his head as he retrieved the puck. "Didn't think you had that in you."

There's a lot you don't know about me, Hayes.

"Lucky shot," Ellis grumbled as he skated past, his voice low enough that only I could hear the comment.

I ignored him, forcing myself to refocus.

But the tension didn't stay verbal. By the time we hit scrimmage drills, Ellis wasn't just running his mouth—he was gunning for me on the ice.

St. James didn't speak. He just skated in, body angled between us, a silent warning in the set of his shoulders.

I caught a clean pass from Rhodes at the blue line and pivoted hard into the offensive zone. Eyes scanning the ice, I threaded the puck between defenders, building speed as I crossed center. That was when I felt it.

A weight slammed into my side, sharp and off angle. It wasn't a legal shoulder check—this was a full shove, dirty and calculated. My balance faltered like a snapped stick, and I crashed into the boards with a hollow, rattling thud. Pain ricocheted up my shoulder and through my ribs. The impact rattled my bones, but the fire in my chest burned hotter.

The hit landed harder than it should have, knocking something loose in my chest—not just air but anger I couldn't shake. Maybe because I hadn't slept much. Maybe because I kept thinking about what my mom had said last night, her voice too steady to be reassuring.

"Your dad's having more bad days than good," she'd admitted quietly. "He asked about your game this weekend."

I should've been focused, should've let it fuel me, but it just felt like one more thing I was failing to handle.

The whistle shrieked sharp and fast, pulling me from my thoughts.

"Ellis!" St. James's roar cracked across the rink like a puck to the glass. He was already skating over, shoving Ellis square in the chest. "What the hell is your problem? You want to fight your teammate or play some damn hockey?"

Ellis smirked, unbothered. "Just making sure the kid can take a hit."

But I saw the flicker of something darker in his eyes. He wanted me rattled, off my game. Not today. I got to my feet, shoving my helmet back into place. "Next time, maybe aim for someone who isn't already past the play."

"Maybe next time, keep your head up, rookie."

My teeth ground together. He didn't know it, but my head was clearer than it had ever been.

Before I could respond, the assistant coach skated over, irritation clear on his face. "That's enough. Ellis, take a lap. Davis, back in rotation."

Ellis skated off, but I could still feel his eyes on me. By the time we got off the ice, I was exhausted—physically and mentally. I sat on the bench, peeling off my gloves, replaying Ellis's earlier words.

Hayes dropped down beside me, stretching out his legs. "You know he's trying to get in your head, right?"

I let out a dry laugh. "Yeah. It's working."

Hayes huffed. "Ignore him. He's been like this since last season. He feels threatened, and instead of stepping up, he just stirs shit."

I nodded, but it didn't make it any easier to let go. Because this wasn't about Ellis, not really. This was about Nyx. The woman who looked at me like she knew too much. Who kept showing up in my thoughts at the worst possible moments, softening the edges I couldn't afford to lose.

It was the way she carried herself, like she'd learned the hard way not to trust anyone, and yet she still showed up. She fought. That did something to me. So did the way she avoided talking about her past but kept letting me in, piece by piece, like she didn't mean to.

And maybe Ellis saw that. Maybe that was why he pushed— because she mattered more to me than she should. Because I wasn't just defending myself or a teammate. I was protecting something I didn't fully understand but wasn't ready to lose.

Later, after I showered and changed, I walked along the hallway that buzzed with low voices and the rhythmic squeak of a cart wheeling past. My head was still running laps, trying to shake the anger Ellis had planted.

It wasn't long before I found myself lingering outside the conference room where Nyx tended to work when she was here. I told myself it was coincidence, but the truth was I needed to see her after Ellis's bullshit. To anchor myself and remember what mattered. My feet had carried me there before my brain could catch up. I hesitated, hand hovering over the door handle, then stepped back.

The door cracked open before I could decide to walk in. Nyx stepped out, tablet in hand, earbuds in. She blinked when she saw me, surprised but not startled.

"Hey." She tugged one bud free.

"Hey." I scrubbed a hand over the back of my neck. "Didn't mean to interrupt."

"You didn't. I needed a break." She tilted her head, eyes scanning my face with quiet curiosity. "You okay?"

"Yeah," I lied then shrugged. "Just needed a second."

She nodded like she understood more than I'd said. "Come on. You look like you could use caffeine and silence. I know just the place."

I followed her down the hall and into one of the staff break rooms tucked near the media offices. The lighting was soft, the hum of the mini fridge the only sound.

She walked straight to the counter and popped a pod into the Nespresso. "You're getting the full assistant experience today," she said, her voice light as the machine hissed to life.

"You don't have to—"

She glanced over her shoulder. "Please. I need the distraction."

I leaned against the counter beside her, watching the steam rise from the little cup.

"I don't know how you drink it black." Her eyebrows rose as she passed me the coffee then inserted another pod and set her mug beneath the spout before pressing the button. "What are you, a federal agent or a masochist?"

I smirked. "It's coffee. Why ruin it?"

She took her cup full of steaming coffee, opened the fridge, grabbed Snickers-flavored creamer, and poured in a heavy dose. "You mean why enjoy it?"

"Looks like dessert."

She took a sip and gave me a pointed look. "Exactly."

I laughed under my breath and let the warmth of the drink and her presence settle some of the static still buzzing in my chest.

"Thanks," I said after a beat. "For this. For… just being here."

Her expression softened. "Anytime."

I studied her face for a moment longer, wondering how I was ever supposed to think of her as just another assistant. She wasn't. She never had been. And if Ellis said another word about her—he would regret it.

CHAPTER TWELVE

NYX

I excused myself after the cup of coffee with Mav to attend a PR meeting to ensure all staff who managed any aspects of the players' lives were on the same page. On my way to the meeting, I cut through the lower hallway that connected the assistant staff rooms to the coaching offices. I wasn't trying to snoop—but when I passed the head coach's office, the voices inside were loud enough to carry.

"You think a handful of decent shifts makes up for weeks of coasting?"

I recognized the head coach's voice.

"You're lucky the press has their eyes on someone else right now. If they were looking here, they'd see an overpaid forward underperforming during a contract year."

I didn't know who said that. Maybe it was one of the assistant coaches.

A pause. Craig's lower voice was muffled, defensive. "You think I don't see what's happening? You're grooming that rookie to take my spot. He hasn't even earned it."

"He doesn't need to earn it, Craig." The head coach didn't miss a beat. "He's already producing."

"It's not just the minutes you're taking from me to give to him," Craig snapped. "The league's watching every step we take after Jennings. And you're gonna hand the spotlight to a kid who has the potential to drag us down in the same way?"

My blood iced. *He's trying to tie Mav in to Jennings's mistakes?*

The head coach didn't flinch. "That kid shows up. He plays clean. He performs. He hasn't done anything to warrant the bullshit you're spewing. You want more time on the ice? Then back it up with solid plays."

The conversation echoed the precariousness of what was at stake. Craig didn't just hate Mav. He saw him as a threat. His resentment wasn't petty. It was desperate. I should've seen it sooner.

During practice, it hadn't been standard checking or heat-of-the-moment scuffles. There'd been aggression to Craig's moves whenever Mav was on the ice—more hits than necessary, slashes that hit too hard or lingered a second too long. I'd written it off as competitiveness. It snapped into focus with painful clarity. Craig wasn't just pissed. He was gunning for Mav consistently, like he was waiting for the moment no one would question him if something went wrong.

It made my stomach knot because I knew how determined Craig could be if he thought he was entitled to something—and how dangerous he was. The sickening truth that Craig wasn't only playing to prove himself but that he was trying to take something from Mav hit me with blunt force. I knew that Craig was afraid. And people who were afraid were unpredictable.

I backed away before they could come out and see me. My chest was tight, my thoughts already spinning as I rushed toward the meeting I would be late for if I didn't get going.

The conference room buzzed with chatter as relevant staff and players' assistants packed up their tablets and stat sheets an hour later. I hovered just outside the frame of it all, trying to keep my head down as I finished taking notes.

One of the media coordinators mumbled something under his breath, and I caught a sliver of it: "Let's just hope we don't get another Jennings situation. That rookie scandal nearly tanked our rep last season."

Someone else grunted. "Yeah. Last thing we need is another new guy screwing around with someone on the staff. PR's still rebuilding from that mess."

Their words hit like a slap. I froze, my feet taking root rather than propelling me out of my chair.

Jennings had been a rookie forward like Mav—promising, reckless, and fast-tracked for stardom until the whole thing imploded. Rumors said he'd gotten involved with someone in marketing. It'd spiraled fast when news hit the press—conflict of interest, power imbalance, front-office drama. That wasn't all. There had been rumors of physical abuse too. They'd tried to clean it up, but the stain stuck.

And now here I was, staff, technically married to Mav.

My grip tightened on my tablet as I backed out of the room. Nobody noticed. Or maybe they did and just didn't say anything. Either way, I felt the warning loud and clear. The line I was walking wasn't just risky. It was dangerous.

On the heels of catching gossip about the far-too-parallel scandal to my secret marriage to my boss, I turned chicken and fled the arena, opting for space instead of checking in with Mav. I told myself it was just for some peace and quiet, but really, it was about breathing without him crowding my every thought. Between practice, weights, meetings, and film, there would be time before he was due home. And I had to go there to work, since my place didn't have electricity—I needed money for luxuries like that.

The condo felt suffocating by the time I wrapped up my tasks for the day. The walls felt like they were shrinking, pressing closer with every second I stayed. I shot Mav a text: *Heading out to run errands. Your dry cleaning is in your closet, meal prepped in the fridge with a note for reheating. If you need anything, just call or text. Got a dentist appointment.*

I didn't. But I wanted a reason to be gone when he got back home, not that he would expect me to be there.

As soon as I left the building, I let out a slow breath and pressed my fingers to my temples, my pulse thrumming against them. My chest ached with the release, as if I'd been holding my breath for hours without realizing it. My thoughts were scattered far and wide but mainly trapped in the complications my stepfamily constantly stirred up.

Cynthia was evil, and her daughter, Trina, was the rotten apple that hadn't fallen far from the tree. So I shouldn't be surprised my stepsister was engaged to a guy as petty and manipulative as she was.

What's Craig's angle? He wasn't the type to play small games. He liked destruction too much to settle for background noise. I knew he was an asshole, but the way he was targeting Mav felt like something more. And Trina... I hadn't even run into her today. While Mav had been out of town visiting his parents over the weekend, I'd gone to that stupid bridal luncheon that had been my bargaining chip with Trina for this job. Four hours of fake compliments and women comparing ring sizes like it was a blood sport. It had been torture but mostly uneventful. At least until the last half hour.

I'd been reaching for a glass of water when had Trina stepped away from Lara, where they'd had their heads together, then slid into the empty seat beside me, all teeth and tight smiles. She waited until the others were deep in conversation about honeymoon packages before leaning in.

"Vegas was wild," she said lightly, glancing briefly in Lara's direction. "I heard from a little birdy that you were seen sneaking off with one of the hockey players. Kind of bold, even for you."

I turned my head slowly. "Excuse me?"

Her eyes sparkled with mock innocence. "No shame in it, sis. You're single. But I do wonder what kind of man doesn't even bother to remember your name after a night like that."

The air vanished from the room, and my pulse thudded in my temples. She didn't know. She couldn't. But she did suspect something, and so did her BFF, Lara.

I forced my tone to stay neutral. "Sounds like your birdy's confusing me with someone else."

Trina laughed, too loud, drawing a few curious glances. "Right. Because you were just so well-behaved that weekend. Come to think of it, you did check out kind of early. And I don't remember seeing the guy you were rumored to be drinking with later either."

I smiled despite the chill racing through my veins. "If you're that desperate for gossip, maybe you should worry about your fiancé."

Her expression faltered enough to satisfy something dark in me.

She recovered quickly. "Craig's not perfect, but at least I know where he sleeps."

I held her gaze. "Do you?"

That shut her up. But even as I'd walked out of that overpriced restaurant, my duty done, I knew I'd given Trina even more cause to sharpen her claws on me, and she wouldn't stop until she'd drawn blood. I just didn't know how much she'd already scented.

I honestly didn't know what was coming, but I could feel something building beneath the surface. And I hated the unknown.

I wished Dad were here. The hollow ache of missing him

carved deeper, sharper in moments like this. He'd been my confidant, the person I'd relied on whenever things were hard. I could almost hear his voice, as if I'd told him about withholding critical information from Mav, the bargain I'd made with the devil—aka Trina—to get this job, and my steadily building debt —God, the debt. Rent was one huge part of it, but I also had massive student loans to pay off. Dad would have given me that understanding smile, slung an arm around my shoulders, and told me nothing was as bad as it seemed. I was a Lawson, after all, and we always came out on top.

But he hadn't come out on top in the end. Not really. And neither had I.

I drove toward the coast, following the familiar route that had always been my escape—the beach, the boardwalk. The sharp scent of salt water hit me first, crisp and clean, a contrast to the murkiness in my mind. The one place that felt like mine. I parked in my usual spot and slipped a few coins into the meter before stepping out and breathing in the salt-heavy air. The wind whipped dark-brown strands of hair across my face as I made my way down the wooden planks, my shoes scuffing against the worn surface.

The boardwalk was quieter than usual—just a few scattered tourists, a couple of kids running ahead of their parents, and an older man playing the guitar by the railing. The usual vendors were out, selling everything from homemade jewelry to funnel cakes. The smells of fried dough and sea salt wrapped around me, and for a moment, I enjoyed the distraction.

I splurged, grabbed a lemonade from a stand near the surf shop, and wandered toward the railing, watching the waves crash against the shore. It was a small rebellion, spending money I didn't technically have, but I needed the comfort. The tide was coming in, rolling higher with each passing minute.

I used to come here with my dad when I was younger. My throat tightened at the memory, the ache settling low in my chest like a weight I couldn't lift. We would get ice cream and sit on the benches, people watching and making up stories about passing strangers. He'd been my safe place, the one person I could count on, and he was gone. The pain in my chest deepened. I'd spent the last few years running from my past, my mistakes, and the truth. Now, I was tangled in lies I wasn't sure I could get out of.

Mav deserved the truth. But telling him would ruin everything. Hope flickered and died in the same breath.

The waves rolled in, steady and unbothered, an endless rhythm that didn't give a damn about my problems. I envied them—the simplicity of the tide, the certainty of its pull. There was something freeing about the waves' indifference. They rose and crashed without caring who they left gasping for air. No lies. No secrets. No impossible choices. But life wasn't that simple.

I reached into my pocket, and my fingers tightened around my phone. I could text Mav right now. My thumb hovered over the contact like it had a mind of its own, craving relief and release all at once. Tell him everything. Tell him why I took the job. Tell him about Cynthia, Trina, Craig, the debt, the months I'd spent barely keeping my head above water, even the marriage certificate I'd found in his Vegas suite with our names on it. I still couldn't recall how we'd gotten it.

Mav was kind. Thoughtful. He'd brought me coffee just because. But if I told him everything, it would all come crashing down. My heart thudded like a ticking clock, counting down to my implosion. The steady trickle of income from this job would keep me afloat. Just a little more time, and I would have enough to pay off the bulk of my rent, enough to keep my landlord off my back and buy the time that I couldn't afford to lose.

Fear was a weight on my shoulders, suffocating me. Mav wouldn't forgive me if I came clean. And even if he somehow did, the damage would be done. I would lose the job and my chance to finally get ahead. He would look at me differently, like I was just another person who'd used him and taken advantage of what he could offer.

Despite the heat of the day, I shivered. Fear rolled beneath my skin, colder than the ocean breeze. I couldn't let that happen. Not when I was this close. I exhaled sharply and shoved my phone back into my pocket. The truth would have to wait.

I stepped back from the railing, from the ocean's steady rhythm and the dangerous clarity that had almost made me crack open. The breeze, salty and sharp, tangled through my hair, tugging like it wanted to pull the truth from me. Laughter floated up from the boardwalk—carefree and hollow. Somewhere nearby, the scent of fried dough and sunscreen lingered, sticky and too sweet, a jarring contrast to the sour churn in my stomach.

Turning away felt like sealing myself in concrete, frozen in time. Like the version of me that had considered telling him was still standing at that rail, waiting for someone braver to take her place. I walked back toward my car, each step heavier than the last, the weight of my choice pressing down like wet sand clinging to my skin. I would keep hiding for now—not because I wanted to but because I didn't know how to survive the fallout if I didn't.

CHAPTER THIRTEEN

NYX

I wasn't sure what had possessed me to agree to this. Maybe I craved the distraction or wanted to see Mav in a way that wasn't tangled with stolen glances and suffocating tension.

Harper, the PR liaison, had shoved the bag of team merchandise into my arms before I'd had a chance to protest. Maybe it was Mav's expectant look, like he'd already assumed I would come along, when he told me he'd roped some guys into joining us at the hospital. Or maybe the idea of seeing him in this setting, surrounded by fans and kids who idolized him, did something weird to my chest. Either way, I was here.

We walked through the hospital's main entrance together, the automatic doors whooshing open. The chill of the air-conditioning pressed against my skin in contrast to the warmth of my buzzing anxiety. Harper had arranged everything—the meet and greet, the photos, the press coverage—but Mav had pushed for the real part of today's visit—the cancer ward.

As we headed down the brightly lit hallways, I glanced at Mav. He looked steady, collected. But I knew where his head had been lately and that this was about more than just PR. His eyes told another story, shadows lingering beneath the surface.

"You ready for this?" I adjusted the bag of hats and jerseys on my shoulder. Part of me wasn't sure if I was asking about the hospital or everything from Vegas that lay unspoken between us.

Mav exhaled, running a hand through his dark hair. "Yeah. Just hope I don't mess it up." His confidence frayed at the edges, revealing the man beneath the armor.

I frowned. "You're just talking to people, signing some jerseys. You can't mess this up."

A slight smirk played on his lips, but it didn't quite reach his eyes. "Yeah? I bet they'll ask why they've never heard of me."

I bumped his shoulder gently. "Then you tell them you're the best-kept secret in the league. Rising star and all that."

He huffed a quiet laugh. "Let's hope they buy it."

We reached the conference room set up for the event, where Kieran, Nick, and a few other players were already inside, posing for photos and signing merch for excited kids and their parents. The hospital staff had gone all out—balloons in team colors, streamers, and an autograph table. The bright decorations felt like a stand against the weight of sickness in the air.

A cluster of kids in oversized Titans jerseys huddled near the table, bouncing excitedly on their toes. A couple of nurses in scrubs hovered nearby, holding clipboards and cell phones, beaming like proud aunts. Kieran knelt beside one of the kids like he'd done it a hundred times, his steady voice putting the boy at ease. Nick signed a puck with a grin.

Mav took a slow breath, rolling his shoulders, then glanced at me. "You coming?"

Something in his voice felt like a tether between us. I nodded. "Yeah. Someone has to make sure you don't traumatize any children."

He laughed then pushed open the door.

The room buzzed with energy. Parents snapped photos while their kids clutched Sharpies and hockey pucks. Harper stood near a local reporter, smiling and talking fast—the woman could spin anything into PR gold.

I made my way through the crowd, pulling hats and shirts from the branded duffel bag. "All right, one item per person! No stealing from your siblings. I will tattle to your moms."

Some of the older kids snorted. An older boy, maybe ten or eleven, with a knitted beanie and a Titans hoodie tugged at my elbow, and I turned to find a wide-eyed face.

"Can I have the blue one?" He pointed at a hat with Mav's jersey number stitched on the side. "It's Davis's favorite color."

I blinked. "It is, huh?"

He nodded solemnly, the nasal tube around his ears catching the light. "He said so in that interview with ESPN when he got drafted."

Damn. He was dedicated.

I handed him the hat. "Tell him that. He'll love it."

The boy grinned then leaned in close. "Will he come see my brother? He's in room three twenty-nine."

My heart ached for him, but I smiled and did my best to hide my sympathy. "Of course he will."

After the event room emptied, a nurse named Carmen met us near the elevators. She was cheerful but probably accustomed to long, emotional days. "We're so excited to have you all here," she told the players. "Some of the kids are in their rooms, but they've been looking forward to this all week. I've got a list and a route."

Mav nodded, stepping forward like he'd done this a dozen times. "We'll follow your lead."

The other guys—including Kieran and Nick—split off with Carmen and a second nurse to handle different floor sections, but Mav asked to go solo. Of course he did. He wasn't here for photo ops. He was here for the kids. I filled him in on the little boy and his brother, who was in room three twenty-nine, then trailed behind him, quiet, the bag of signed merch slung over my shoulder.

Each room was its own quiet world. Monitors beeped like steady heartbeats, a fragile reminder of life inside thin walls. The lights were dimmed with family members perched at bedsides. Some kids had visitors. Others didn't.

But every single one lit up when Mav walked through the door, like he carried the sunlight in his wake, banishing the shadows for a moment.

He didn't rush. He crouched beside each bed, made eye contact, and asked questions that weren't about being sick. He talked about hockey, cracked jokes, and even reenacted a slow-motion version of one of his goals from a game last season for a kid too tired to laugh—but who smiled anyway.

There were no cameras, no reporters. Just him and them—and me, on the outside looking in, watching a man who was so much more than the headlines ever captured. At one point, he leaned over to help a boy adjust his pillows so he could sit up straighter.

Another time, he signed a cast already covered in messages —his carefully scrawled *#27 Mav Davis* squeezed between *get well soon* and a crude drawing of a dinosaur. In the doorway, I caught a mom quietly wiping away tears. My throat thickened, the weight of love and fear in that mother's eyes achingly familiar. Mav noticed, too, and his smile faltered for just a second before he turned back to the boy and whispered something that made him laugh so hard his IV monitor beeped in protest. The nurses watched from the hallway, nodding, whispering to each other like he'd just moved up in their internal hero rankings.

Finally, we reached the brother of the boy we'd met earlier. He lay in his bed, his dad sitting beside him, one hand resting protectively on his son's wrist, his fingers tense as if he could anchor his son to the world by sheer will.

The young boy next to the bed, who we'd learned was Charlie, beamed the second Mav stepped inside. "You came!" he whispered, hugging the blue hat.

"Of course." Mav crouched beside the bed like it was the most natural thing in the world. "I couldn't leave my best fans hanging, could I?"

The sick boy lying in bed laughed. "Did you bring the team?"

"Some of them." Mav glanced at me. "But I saved the best visit for last."

Charlie looked past Mav and gave me a little wave. I smiled and returned it, though my throat was too tight to speak.

"You doing okay?" Mav gently tapped the sick boy's wristband with one knuckle.

He nodded. "Better now."

The family gushed about watching Mav play in college, following his career path along with those of many others from Fall Lake University. They talked a bit longer—about the sick boy's favorite player, Mav; his second-favorite player, who was a goalie from a rival team, which earned a fake gasp from Mav; and his dream to skate again once he was out of the hospital.

Mav promised he would have a pair of skates with the boy's name on them waiting at the arena when he was ready. It wasn't just a promise. It was hope, offered like a lifeline. I could see the emotion flicker across his dad's face—gratitude and heartbreak rolled into one.

We thanked the staff, even more of whom had joined to chat with the players who were finishing up. Just then, a nurse stepped into view at the far end of the hallway, her scrubs neat and her expression a little too curious. I froze.

It took a beat to place her, but when I did, my stomach flipped—Lara Winthrop, aka "Kate Upton" from Trina's Vegas bachelorette party. ER nurse and full-fledged member of the bitch squad my stepsister surrounded herself with like a designer security blanket.

She'd helped plan that entire Hollywood glam weekend,

always hovering near the center of attention. She hadn't changed much—still polished, calculating, and looking like she kept a running scoreboard on everyone in the room. And, apparently, she worked here.

Her gaze landed on me and lingered for half a second too long. I quickly looked away but not before I caught the whisper she passed to the nurse beside her, followed by a pointed glance at Mav. Alarm bells rang in my head. I made a note to mention it to him later, but I didn't want to ruin the moment for the kids.

"Well, if it isn't the Titans doing good deeds. Shame I didn't get the memo." The voice, too familiar and too smug, echoed from the hallway.

Craig strolled in like he owned the place, casual in a bomber jacket and jeans, but with eyes scanning for a camera. My stomach dipped. Lara's face lit up just a bit too brightly.

"What the hell are you doing here?" I whispered as he neared.

Craig shrugged like it was nothing. "Heard about the charity signing through the grapevine. Figured I'd stop in, make it even more special." He shot a smirk at Mav. "Wouldn't want the rookie to get overwhelmed."

Mav's jaw ticked. I folded my arms, schooling my features. "Funny. Didn't realize this was public knowledge."

Craig's grin widened as he glanced past me toward Lara. "Word travels. Good to see some familiar faces, huh?"

Lara gave a little wave, playing innocent. I caught the way her eyes darted to Craig's, and something in the exchange made my skin crawl. It was too comfortable, too familiar.

Mav stepped forward slightly, his presence suddenly towering. "We're finishing up," he said tightly.

Craig's gaze flicked to him, amused. "Didn't mean to interrupt. Just thought I'd show support. PR loves that kinda stuff, right?" He didn't wait for an answer before striding toward the next room with Lara at his heels.

I worked to push the moment with Craig and Lara from my mind and enjoy the incredible thing Mav had done. That was worth dwelling over, not a small blip in our day.

The sun was setting as we pulled out of the hospital parking lot. The weight of the visit sat between us, unspoken but heavy.

"You needed that, too, didn't you?" I finally asked, breaking the silence.

Mav's eyes stayed on the road. "Yeah. I did." His admission felt like an unguarded truth, raw and real.

"Was it about your dad?"

His hands tightened slightly on the wheel. "Yeah."

I nodded, watching the city blur past the window. Lights smeared into gold-and-white streaks, mirroring my swirling thoughts. "You gave those kids something real today, something that didn't have to do with being sick."

He didn't answer right away. When he finally spoke, his voice was low. "I just… I know what it's like to feel powerless—when my sister died and again with Dad's cancer."

I glanced at him, at the profile of a guy who most people only saw on the ice. "You gave those kids something to fight for. That matters."

The tension in his shoulders eased just a little. "Maybe I needed that reminder too."

"You think you'll visit again?"

"Yeah," he said without hesitation. "Next time, I'm bringing more hats." His mouth curved into the hint of a smile.

I studied him, seeing him not as the guy tied to a mess I couldn't untangle but as a man quietly carrying the weight of his grief and still finding room to lift others. He was steady and selfless. He made it hard to keep my walls intact, hard to pretend this was just a job.

I grinned. "And maybe more patience for the kids who know your stats better than you."

He shot me a look. "You enjoyed that way too much."

"You're damn right I did."

And for a moment, the weight of it all—the season, the media, my pseudo-family, and the things we weren't saying—rose, just a little. It was like breathing without pain or catching a glimpse of clear sky in a storm.

CHAPTER FOURTEEN

NYX

I left Harper's office at the arena and headed toward the exit. My exhaustion was bone-deep, fatigue that no amount of caffeine or sleep could relieve. Every day felt like treading water in a storm, each task another wave threatening to pull me under. Between work, the financial stress that never eased, and the ever-present paranoia of Mav figuring out the truth, I was running on fumes.

Still, I shouldn't be this run-down. It had to be stress. The alternative of what I'd lived through with my dad's cancer happening to me was too terrifying to consider. So I wouldn't think it. Stress was the only explanation. I wasn't sleeping well, I was hardly eating, and I was constantly moving to keep up with everything. Things would improve once I paid my rent and the eviction threat hanging over my head disappeared. And I was close—just one week to go until I put down a payment.

The hospital visit yesterday had been a success. But even that fleeting sense of accomplishment had been drowned by today's weight. Harper had given me a few other dates to figure into Mav's calendar for future charity events. She'd even commented on how tired I looked, which was a clear sign I needed to leave, do my errands, then go home and get some rest. My reflection in the glass door earlier had confirmed it—hollow eyes, tight skin, a shadow of the girl I used to be.

As I passed the staff hallway near the media office, I heard a familiar smug voice float from one of the open doorways.

"She's only here still because Mav hasn't come to his senses yet," Trina said, her tone clipped and defensive. "Craig's taking all the heat for the locker-room tension, but he's not the one they should be worried about."

I slowed just enough to catch the rest, my breath stalling.

"First Jennings, now this? Another rookie with poor impulse control falling for the first girl who batted her lashes in Vegas?" Trina laughed lightly. "They'll spin it like a fairy tale, but we all know it's a ticking time bomb."

Someone murmured something too soft to hear, and Trina scoffed. "Honestly, they're lucky it hasn't exploded already."

My throat tightened. I kept walking, faster now, before Trina saw me—before I could hear anything else that would wedge deeper beneath my skin.

The arena was cool, the air humming with the steady sounds of weights clanking and muffled conversation as I neared the weight room, where most of the team was finishing their session.

I turned the corner, adjusting my bag on my shoulder. The strap dug deep like a constant reminder of the burden I carried. Social media to update, errands to run, and whatever last-minute tasks Mav needed to have taken care of for the rest of the day occupied my mind. I barely had time to react before a figure stepped into my path, blocking my way—Craig. My pulse jumped, a cold jolt running down my spine at the sight of him. He must've wrapped up early.

I stiffened instinctively, my grip tightening around the strap of my bag. He leaned against the wall, arms crossed over his chest, wearing that smug, self-satisfied smirk that made me want to punch him.

His gaze flicked over me, slow and deliberate, and my stomach churned. I fought the urge to shrink away, to shield myself from how his eyes turned my skin to ice. *How long will he wait to cheat on Trina after they get married?* If he wasn't already.

"I could use a personal assistant." His words slithered like poison wrapped in velvet. "When're you gonna dump Davis and start assisting me?"

A few feet to the side of Craig, Logan Reeves watched from the doorway of the gym, doing nothing to help.

I shoved past my soon-to-be brother-in-law, refusing to let him intimidate me. Every step away a victory, reclaiming a sliver of control as I tossed a response over my shoulder. "When hell freezes over, buddy."

His chuckle followed me down the hall, low and taunting. "I'll be waiting."

I picked up my pace, needing to get as far away from him as possible. I was used to his lingering glances and suggestive comments by now, but he was getting more aggressive—and that was a situation I didn't want to experience ever again. My body felt rigid, my hands trembling slightly at my sides, but I didn't stop until I reached the exit. The cool air hit me like a slap, sharp and jarring, and I sucked in a deep breath—then the dizziness hit. The floor tilted beneath me. My knees wobbled as nausea surged fast and hot.

It crashed over me. My vision blurred, and my stomach lurched violently. I stumbled to the nearest trash can before everything inside me came up in harsh, gut-wrenching waves. I clutched the edge of the bin, chest heaving, my body trembling from the force of it.

This wasn't just stress. Dread curled under my ribs, twisting my insides in knots. Realization hit me like a freight train—something was wrong.

My first instinct was to call Mav, not out of obligation, just because he'd become the person I wanted in my corner. And that realization hit harder than the dizziness. Because maybe those feelings were exactly what would make calling him in these circumstances the wrong choice. It would be unprofessional to rely on him for emotional support. No, I needed to pull myself together.

CHAPTER FIFTEEN

MAV

The neighborhood ice arena where a junior high team was due to practice smelled like old ice and sharpened skates, the kind of scent that had been ingrained in me since I was a kid, grounding me in comfort and familiarity. It wasn't an NHL facility, nothing state-of-the-art—just a local rink filled with energy. The kind that reminded me why I'd fallen in love with the game in the first place.

Nyx stood beside me at the boards. She looked tired, worn around the edges with her arms crossed, but her eyes held a spark as she watched a handful of little kids finish their short learn-to-skate session. Even when she was running on fumes, there was something steady about her—she wouldn't give in. Regardless of how determined and strong she was, I would keep an eye on her, just to make sure she was okay.

The ice was littered with tiny skaters finishing up—another few minutes, and the kids shuffled off toward their parents. Just beyond the glass, another group of kids waited—older, restless, and eager for their turn.

"You do this often?" Nyx asked, her voice light, but I caught the curiosity behind it.

"When I can." My answer came easy, even if she didn't know how much I needed this more than anyone else here. I rested my forearms on the boards, glancing at her before looking back at the ice. "It's easy to get caught up in everything—training, games, pressure. But this? This keeps things in perspective."

One of the little kids lost their footing and hit the ice hard. Before the instructor could reach her, I glided over.

"Need a hand?" I crouched, holding out my gloved palm.

Wide-eyed, she blinked up at me before hesitantly reaching for me. "I keep falling."

I helped her find her balance. "First rule of skating?" I told her, squeezing her tiny mitten in mine. "Falling's a part of it. You just get back up and try again. Every time." And hell, that was the same rule I'd been living by off the ice as well with my sister's passing and my dad's illness.

She gave a determined nod, her little legs still shaky, but she gripped my hand tighter as I helped her push forward. The younger kids were off the ice a few minutes later, and the next group was ready.

My phone buzzed in my pocket. I didn't need to check the screen. I already knew it was Mom. She called every week after Dad's appointments, even when there was nothing new to say.

I swiped the screen and pressed the phone to my ear. "How is he?"

Her sigh said it all. "Tired. More pain than usual. They adjusted the meds again."

I closed my eyes briefly. "Okay. Let me know if you need help with anything."

"Just play well in your next game," she said. "He watches every one."

Guilt gnawed at me. I'd been so focused on Ellis and everything going wrong here, I hadn't checked in the way I should've. We chatted for another minute or two before I told her I had to go and why.

The junior high players flooded onto the rink, their excitement buzzing. Their coach gave me a nod, and I clapped my hands together.

"All right, guys." He clapped a kid on the shoulder. "Let's see what we're working with. Eyes on Davis—if he says jump, you ask how high."

The next hour flew by. I ran drills with them, fine-tuning their movements, offering pointers on their wrist shots and puck control. The team was decent, raw, but hungry, and a few of them had serious potential. Their energy was contagious, bringing me back to when I was just a kid trying to prove myself. Watching them lit something in my chest that I hadn't felt in a while. Pure love of the game. No pressure. No bullshit. Just joy.

When I glanced back toward the stands, I saw Nyx talking to a group of parents. My eyes found hers before I even realized I was looking for her. The headshots she'd brought were neatly stacked and ready while she listened to the parents' questions. She wasn't just standing by. She was making sure they left with something tangible. She looked so damn natural at it—too natural, as if she wasn't just fitting into my life, she was slipping under my skin like my world belonged tangled around hers.

When the session ended, I found myself next to her as a line of kids formed, eager to get something signed. Nyx stood patiently beside me, a quiet, steady presence as I scrawled my name across each headshot, taking the time to talk to the kids, to hear them out.

When the last one ran off, bouncing on their feet as they showed their parents their autographed picture, I turned to Nyx.

"You didn't have to do all that." My voice was lower than I intended. "But I'm glad you did." Damn if I didn't like watching her there, being part of it.

She shrugged, a small smile on her lips. "You were giving

them your time. Figured I'd make sure they got something to take home."

The drive back to my condo was quiet at first, only the road noise filling the silence between us.

Then Nyx shifted in her seat, turning toward me. "What made you choose hockey?"

The question caught me off guard, cutting through the silence and landing harder than it should've. I kept my eyes on the road, my grip on the wheel tightening slightly. "I needed this sport when I was younger," I admitted.

She tilted her head. "What do you mean?"

I hesitated, but then I saw the kids' faces in my mind, how they looked so excited and free. I exhaled. The words scraped out of me, raw. "My sister died when I was nine." And some days, it was as if I were still that kid trying to skate fast enough to outrun the memory.

Nyx stiffened beside me, her sharp inhalation barely audible, but she didn't say anything—just let me talk.

"She was a year older. My parents... They never really recovered. And I didn't know how to deal with it either. But hockey..." I flexed my fingers around the steering wheel. "It gave me something to hold onto. Something that made sense when nothing else did." I let out a dry chuckle. "I wasn't even good when I started—just a scrawny kid with too much energy and big emotions that I took out on a puck. But my coaches saw something. It helped me channel it. And once I realized I had a shot at going somewhere with it, I didn't stop."

Nyx's voice was softer when she spoke. "And now you're here."

I glanced at her. Here didn't feel far enough from then. My hands tightened on the steering wheel again—tight enough that the leather creaked beneath my grip. I forced myself to loosen it one finger at a time. No use choking the wheel just because her words hit harder than I expected.

She nodded slowly, her gaze lingering on me before returning to the window. "I think your sister would be proud."

The simple words punched straight into my chest, sharp enough to leave a mark. I swallowed against it, keeping my focus on the road. "Yeah. Maybe."

For a long moment, neither of us spoke. The quiet between us didn't feel heavy or uncomfortable. It just felt... easy.

CHAPTER SIXTEEN

MAV

I tossed my gear bag onto the floor by the counter and then rolled my shoulders as I stalked toward the office space I'd delegated for Nyx. She had left earlier, to run errands. I hadn't seen her since, but her laptop and a stack of folders sat neatly on the desk, her usual orderliness on display.

Something about her lately had been off, though—more than usual. Like she was unraveling beneath the surface, and I'd been too damn distracted with my dad's health issues to pull at the thread.

Dragging a hand through my hair, I reached for one of the folders and flipped it open out of habit more than curiosity. My gaze snagged on a crumpled piece of paper wedged between the pages. Frowning, I smoothed it out.

My breath locked in my chest. Marriage Certificate. My name. Nyx's name. Signed. Official. Legal. It hit like a truck I never saw coming—my world tilting off its axis before I could brace for impact. The ink might've dried, but nothing about it seemed real. It felt like being sucker punched by a three-week-old memory I didn't even have.

A sick twist coiled in my gut, heat flashing through me so

fast it blurred my vision. My grip tightened around the paper, crinkling the edges. *What the hell is this? Some kind of trick? A scam?*

I stared at it like it might morph into something else if I looked long enough. But the details remained the same. Our names. Our signatures. The date. Vegas.

Then, like a dam cracking wide open, it all came rushing back. The pink dress, the wild lights of Vegas, the way she'd moved in my arms like we were the only two people in the world. *Margot Robbie?* No. *Nyx.* It had been her all along.

Memories tore through me with brutal clarity. My mouth on hers, her laughter in my ear, her hands in my hair as I pressed her against the wall of that goddamn hotel suite. The feel of her legs tightening around my waist. The way we'd burned together, reckless and raw like nothing else existed.

But marriage?

A savage pulse thundered in my ears. *What the hell is she playing at? Was this her game all along? Some insurance policy she'd kept tucked away, waiting to cash in?*

The condo door opened behind me, her footsteps light across the floor.

"Mav?" Nyx's voice was casual, like my entire life hadn't just been turned on its side.

I stepped into the hallway with the paper clutched so tightly in my fist, my knuckles ached. She froze the second she saw it. Her eyes widened, her face draining of color like she'd seen a ghost.

"What the hell is this?" I bit out, holding the certificate up like an accusation.

Her throat bobbed as she swallowed. "Mav, I—"

"When were you planning to tell me, exactly?" I cut her off, my pulse spiking with each word. I stalked closer, heat roaring under my skin. "Or were you just hoping I would never find out? Thought you'd keep it tucked away like a get-out-of-jail-free card?"

"I didn't know how to tell you," she said, her voice tight, defensive.

"How about you start with the truth?" My words cracked like a whip. "That's usually a damn good place to begin."

Her arms crossed over her chest, her posture stiffening, but something flickered in her eyes. *Regret? Fear?* I couldn't tell.

"I didn't remember the ceremony in Vegas," she admitted, her voice wavering. "Not at first."

A sharp, humorless laugh ripped from my throat. "Not at first? But you do now. Don't you?"

"Bits and pieces," she whispered, her blue-green gaze dropping to the floor like it hurt to meet my eyes.

"So, what?" My voice rose, frustration clawing at my chest. "You kept it in your back pocket, waiting for the right moment to spring it on me? Hoping I'd never notice? Just waiting to ride out your little payday?"

"That's not what this is," she snapped, her fists curling at her sides. "I was trying to figure it out, just like you are now. I was going to get it annulled. I still am."

My jaw clenched so tight my teeth ached. "And you thought you'd just erase it like it never happened? Handle it on your own? You didn't think I deserved to know?"

Her lips parted, but her breath caught before the words could come. "I know it looks bad," she finally said, her voice softening just enough to splinter something in me. "I panicked. Then I tried to focus on the job because it was all I could control. I need this job, Mav. Desperately. I wasn't trying to trap you." She hesitated, a beat too long, panic flickering in her expression. "Just know it wasn't about you. It was never about you. My family... They're complicated. I cashed in on a debt my stepsister owed me for attending an event they wanted me to go to. That's all."

"Convenient timing," I growled, stepping closer until there was barely a breath between us. Her family wasn't my concern at the moment—our situation was. "So, tell me something, Nyx. If you weren't planning on trapping me, why the hell are you still here?"

Her chin rose, defiance flashing in her eyes. "Because I'm good at my job. And I was trying to do it right. I figured if I kept things professional and maintained my distance, it wouldn't matter. I could... pretend it never happened."

"Pretend?" I echoed, my voice rough. "Secrets always find a way of coming out."

"I wasn't going to keep it from you forever," she added, her voice rising. "I wasn't even sure it was real at first. I thought maybe it was some joke, something forged. I didn't remember everything, and by the time the memories returned—"

"You were already in too deep," I finished for her bitterly.

She shook her head. "No, I was trying to fix it. I started the paperwork for the annulment the day after I got back. But they needed both parties, Mav. Your signature. And after that night, I didn't know where to find you until I landed this job with the Titans."

"So why not bring it up the second we saw each other?" I demanded. "Why not tell me once we were alone?"

"Because, by then, everything had changed. You had so much on the line—your career and your dad's health. I didn't want this—us—to become a PR nightmare. Or worse, something that could derail everything for both of us."

My breath caught. Her voice, her face... She meant it. She hadn't been hiding it to trap me. She'd been scared of blowing up my life.

I dropped my hand to my side, the paper still clenched in my fist. "So where does that leave us?"

"I still plan to get the annulment," she said, quieter now. "I just... I was waiting. I figured we'd get through the season. Keep our heads down. No headlines. Then end it quietly. We're not pretending it didn't happen. We're making sure it doesn't destroy anything else."

I stared at her, at the fire in her eyes, the steadiness in her voice, and it hit me—she wasn't the problem. The secret was. But we were in it together now.

The tension between us stretched tight, fraying at the edges until it was ready to snap. Her breath hitched, her chest rising and falling as she fought whatever war raged inside her. I lost the battle first, the erotic images of us in that hotel room blurring time. I caught her wrist, my grip firm but not harsh, and she didn't pull away. Her eyes locked on mine, heat simmering in their depths beneath the panic.

"You want to pretend? Fine," I rasped. "But we both know this is real."

The distance between us vanished. My mouth crashed onto hers, hard and hungry. Her lips parted with a soft gasp. Her hands braced against my chest, but instead of pushing me away, she fisted the front of my shirt and pulled me closer.

Our kiss turned wild, a clash of frustration and something far more dangerous. I backed her toward the wall, crowding her space, my hands dragging down her sides to her hips. She arched into me, her body a perfect match against mine.

We broke apart only to breathe, panting, desperate, the air between us thick with everything we hadn't said. I cupped her jaw and dragged my thumb along her cheek, and she leaned into it like it hurt not to.

"You drive me insane," I whispered against her lips.

"Right back at you," she breathed. "So do something about it."

Clothes came off in a tangle of breathless urgency. My hands roamed her skin like I couldn't get enough, as if I wanted to memorize every inch. And maybe I did.

I carried her into the bedroom, dropped her gently onto the

bed, and followed her down like she was gravity and I didn't want to fight the pull. Her nails scored my back as I lifted her, her legs wrapping around my waist with a familiarity that burned through me.

"Mav," she breathed against my mouth, her voice trembling.

"Don't you dare tell me to stop," I growled, my forehead pressed to hers.

"I won't," she whispered. "I can't."

It was reckless. It was inevitable. And it was the best damn mistake of my life.

Her breath fanned against mine, warm and unsteady. The soft fibers of the sheets bunched around my knees, grounding me as her scent wrapped around me—citrus and something faintly floral, like summer clinging to winter's edge.

Her body pressed against mine, all heat and contradiction. The air between us thickened with every kiss, every gasp. Her skin tasted like defiance, and I drank in every sound she made, storing them like evidence. Proof that she was real. We moved with a desperation that didn't feel new—it felt inevitable.

We moved like we'd done this a hundred times. Like we were made to fit this way. The heat between us scorched away any doubt, any fear, until there was nothing but need.

I kissed her hard. Her fingers tangled in my hair, tugging until I groaned. I slid lower, teasing her thighs apart, and kissed down the length of her body until I could taste her. She gasped, thighs trembling as my tongue swept across her center in long, relentless strokes. I licked, sucked, tormented until she was shaking beneath me, her hips grinding up like she didn't care if we ever stopped. Her voice cracked on my name as she shattered against my mouth, all heat and fury and surrender.

I didn't wait. I rose over her, pulled her flush against me, and kissed her like I'd lost every bit of control. Her hands slipped down, wrapped around me, and guided me exactly where she needed me. I thrust inside in one long, deep slide.

She cried out, her back arching, nails clawing my shoulders as I set a rhythm that grew more desperate by the second. Every thrust was a collision—of anger, need, and something far more dangerous. She was everything—tight and wet and wild beneath me, and I lost myself in her as her hips met mine without hesitation.

She whispered my name like it meant something. I buried my face in her neck, anchoring myself to the sounds she made, to the way her body clung to mine. Her legs locked tight around my hips, urging me deeper, harder, until she clenched around me, broken and wild. I followed her over the edge with a growl, pouring every ounce of fury and want into her until there was nothing left but the sound of our hearts crashing together.

I collapsed onto her before shifting my weight. We were tangled and slick with sweat, her breath rushing against my neck. I didn't say a word. I didn't have to. It was more than lust. We'd just burned everything down to finally see it. We were both breathless, tangled together on the bed like a storm that had finally spent itself.

But she was the first to move, scrambling to gather her clothes. "This changes nothing," she said, her voice tight as she shoved her arms into her shirt. "What I said earlier—I meant it. I'll figure out the annulment. I let things slide because I was trying to do my best job as an assistant. It wasn't to trap you. Never to trap you."

I sat up slowly, my gaze locked on her. "Then why didn't you tell me? Why hide it if you weren't trying to hold this over me?"

"I was scared," she admitted, her eyes bright with unshed tears. "I needed this job more than my pride, and I thought I could fix the mistake before you ever had to know. But... I needed your signature, and I didn't want to cause any negative headlines for you either."

Her words hit me harder than I wanted to admit. "Nyx," I

said, my voice rough. "You can keep telling yourself this was a mistake. But I know better, *wife*."

Her lips parted, her breath stalling. She hesitated at the door, glancing back at me like she wanted to say something else—anything else. But she didn't. She left me there, my pulse still racing, the taste of her kiss lingering on my lips.

I'd thought I would never see my mystery starlet again. Add in the heated argument, the shocking news, and the invasion of memories from the best sex of my life, and what had just happened felt inevitable. I guess that ruled out an annulment, and surprisingly, I wasn't upset about it. There was no way I would sign the paperwork after what we'd experienced together.

CHAPTER SEVENTEEN

NYX

The Titans' payroll email dropped into my inbox just after nine a.m. I opened it with fingers already clammy, breath caught somewhere between hope and dread. Prorated, just like HR had said. Not the full amount. But enough to stop the freefall. Enough to show I wasn't just spinning my wheels anymore.

I hurried to my bank, withdrew what I could in cash, shoved the bills into a battered envelope, and headed for my apartment building. The cracked stairs echoed under my boots as I climbed the stairwell toward the landlord's office, nerves wound tight. I knocked once—hesitant but firm.

The door swung open before I could knock again. Mr. Harnois squinted at me like I'd interrupted his coffee. The lines on his face mapped out his age with alarming accuracy. His white caterpillar eyebrows furrowed, and I did my best to ignore the hair curling over the V of his tired navy T-shirt collar.

"Nyx," he said, voice gravelly. "You got it all this time?"

This wasn't the first time I'd made a small payment, but I held out the envelope just the same, hoping for a better outcome than last time—which had earned me no promises on the eviction. "Not the full amount. It's half. My first paycheck hit this morning. The next one will be bigger."

He didn't take it right away. He just looked at me for a second then finally plucked the envelope from my hand, opened the envelope, and counted the bills with deliberate slowness. His brow furrowed. "You're still behind."

"I know. But I'll have the rest in two weeks. I've got a steady job now—with the Titans." I forced myself to hold eye contact. "I'm not avoiding rent. I'll catch up, like I said I would."

Harnois grunted but didn't look convinced. "You said that last time too."

"And I meant it then. I mean it now. I'm not screwing you over, I swear. Just… give me until the next check hits. Then I'll be square."

He sighed, a sound more tired than angry, and pinched the bridge of his nose. "You've bought yourself two more weeks. That's it. If I don't have the full remainder by then, you're out."

I swallowed hard. "Understood."

"No more partials. No more promises. No more texts about 'just a few more days.' I've been patient."

"I know. And I appreciate it," I said quietly.

He stared for another beat then nodded once. "You pay up, and we don't have a problem. You miss it again? That's it. No notice. No grace."

The door clicked shut before I could respond. I stood in the stairwell, staring at the peeling paint and rusted banister. My pulse thundered in my ears, but a different fear had settled in. The clock was ticking. One final window before the floor vanished completely.

The time it had taken to get the money then plead with my landlord made it necessary to go straight to the arena rather than work in my office at Mav's place. I could've used the quiet, some time to settle into the day.

After last night with Mav, I'd barely slept, tossing and turning in tangled sheets. My skin still held the ghost of his touch. His hands had been everywhere, branding me, and the space beside me felt cold in contrast. His expression after—conflicted, unreadable—had twisted in my chest, bleeding me of any certainty.

Not only that, but he'd called me "wife." The sound of it was possessive and hot as hell. *But a future together?* I wasn't sure if I was reading into things.

Desperate for a distraction, I dragged myself to his practice, phone in hand, to get some social media shots like I hadn't completely unraveled beneath him hours earlier. I told myself it was just work—just routine. But my heart was a drumbeat of nerves as I stepped inside the arena, bracing for the inescapable.

And sure enough, I barely made it past the first hallway before I collided with him, the moment awkward and inevitable as gravity. Of course, we bumped into each other in the hall, and I barely made it through our brief interaction without falling apart. My smile felt brittle, my voice thinner than ice about to crack.

I tried to stay busy so the mess in my head and heart would remain quiet. I hightailed it to the lounge, where I buried myself in work, handling everything he needed before asking. *Just keep your head down.* That was what I needed to live by. My fingers tightened around the laptop until my knuckles ached as I pretended everything was normal—it wasn't. When his gaze brushed over me, heat prickled beneath my skin, my mind involuntarily replaying the way his breath had scraped my ear, the weight of his body over mine, the way he'd said my name like it meant something.

Every glance was a silent question I didn't dare answer. His gaze wasn't just assessing—it was dissecting, like he was trying to peel me back to the bone and see if anything was real beneath the mess I'd made. Even if we'd shared a passionate moment together, I knew he was still furious. I knew he didn't trust me. And worst of all, I knew he was waiting for an explanation I didn't know how to give.

The arena lounge was supposed to be a neutral space where the team's significant others could relax, grab a coffee, or wait for practice to end. But right now, it felt like enemy territory. Their words always cut deeper when coated with fake smiles and overpriced lip gloss. It wasn't just the words. It was the way the people wore cruelty like a designer accessory, flashing it right along with their bleached white teeth and their diamond-studded laughs.

I was seated at one of the high-top tables, laptop open, pretending to be busy. But it was impossible to ignore the conversation just a few feet away. Trina and some other girl-friends weren't even trying to be discreet.

"Honestly, I don't know why she even shows her face here," Trina said.

Heat crawled up my neck, a slow, suffocating burn that twisted into a knot of fury lodged beneath my ribs—shame, sharp and bitter, coiled like a serpent in my throat. I forced myself to keep typing, even as my stomach twisted. I braced, expecting the worst.

"I guess it pays to be in the right bed at the right time," one of them added, her voice dripping with mock innocence.

A shrill laugh sounded. "She must be thrilled if they're really hooking up—getting knocked up is the ultimate job security."

My pulse hammered in my ears, drowning out everything but their voices, every syllable slicing through me like paper cuts that wouldn't stop bleeding.

Madison flicked her glossy hair back with a sneer. "You should know, Tonya."

"Shut up—it paid off, didn't it? Still, I was his girlfriend. I put in the time."

"You mean the blow jobs." Madison cackled, too busy making duck lips for a selfie to look in my direction.

"Whatever, you know what I mean. She shouldn't be here." Tonya planted her fists on her curvy hips. Her desperation nearly screamed from her posture despite how she clearly played backup to Trina. "She's basically a puck bunny, not a WAG."

I gritted my teeth, my fingers curling into fists beneath the table. Let them laugh. Let them sneer. I wasn't going to give them the damn satisfaction of seeing me crumble. My stepsister fueled their venom. I'd overheard Trina whisper a few choice things about me in their ears to make sure I wasn't welcome. She might have given me a job when I'd twisted her arm, but she sure as shit didn't want me here and wasn't above using any underhanded method to force me to quit or be exiled in any other manner. I wasn't going to give them the satisfaction of reacting.

"You know, I've never understood the whole jersey-chaser thing," Trina mused, her tone light, casual—like she was discussing the weather. "But I guess some women just have no shame."

Enough. She didn't fucking dare. I wasn't targeting Mav— that was my bitch stepmom and Trina's MO rolled into one. I turned, ready to end this, when another voice cut through the air.

"Wow. The insecurity in this room is suffocating," Vivi snapped. She strolled up to the table like she belonged there— because she did—her expression cool, unimpressed.

Selene was right behind her, her silver cuff bracelet glinting in the light as she crossed her arms, eyes narrowed in challenge. Reinforcements. Relief crashed through me, sharp and unexpected, leaving my knees weak beneath the table. For the first time today, I wasn't alone in this war zone.

Trina stiffened, but her smirk didn't waver. "Oh, look. The welcoming committee."

Vivi tilted her head, feigning confusion. "Oh, were we supposed to be welcoming? Because I was going for bored."

Selene leaned in slightly, voice dropping just enough to sound vaguely threatening. "Might want to be careful, Trina. All that jealousy is starting to show."

Trina snorted. "Please. No one's jealous of a glorified assistant."

Vivi let out a dramatic sigh. "And yet, here you are. Obsessed." She turned to me, ignoring Trina completely. "Come on, Nyx. We don't hang out with the trash."

Selene shot the group one last look before following Vivi's lead. I hesitated then slowly shut my laptop and stood. Walking away felt like a victory.

As I passed Trina, she muttered, "This isn't over."

I didn't look back. "No. But you are."

Vivi grinned as we stepped into the hallway. "God, I love shutting her up."

Selene looped her arm through mine, squeezing me. "Get used to it, friend," she said with a wink. "You're one of us now."

The words were a lifeline I hadn't realized I was reaching for. Belonging. Foreign but achingly sweet. The knots in my stomach loosened just a little. Maybe I wasn't as alone on this battlefield as I'd convinced myself I was. But even surrounded, I still felt like one wrong step would send me back into isolation.

"So, how do you know Trina anyway?" Vivi asked.

Panic flooded my senses as I debated answering honestly, before I gave a tight-lipped response. "We're family. Unfortunately."

Vivi's eyebrows rose, and Selene muttered, "Well, that explains a lot."

"And whatever Trina spits out, her lackeys swallow without question," Vivi added, her eyes narrowing.

Selene scoffed. "One of them used to be a puck bunny. The other was halfway out the door before she probably promised her guy a lifetime supply of blow jobs." She gave a sharp, satisfied smile. "Not exactly moral high ground."

By midafternoon, I decided to step out for some air. Practice in the rink had ended. The guys would be in the weight room or watching film. The arena hallways were mostly empty, and I took a deep breath, trying to calm my racing thoughts. A familiar voice sent a cold shiver down my spine just as I turned the corner.

Craig was leaning against the wall, talking to a couple of the defensemen, his smirk as smug as ever. Poison in a perfectly tailored suit or hockey jersey—it was all the same on him. My stomach clenched on instinct, my fight-or-flight sparking even before he spoke. My gut churned at the sight of him, but it wasn't until I heard my name that I started to pay attention.

"Nepotism at its finest," Craig sneered. "Funny how having a sister like Trina opens the right doors. Wonder what you had to promise to get Davis thrown in as a bonus prize."

Laughter. A couple of the guys said nothing, but I could feel their unease. Craig was testing the waters, seeing who he could turn against me.

My fingers curled into fists. This wasn't happening. Rage pulsed through my veins, hot and blinding. I stepped forward, forcing my voice to stay even. "You have something to say to me, Craig?" My voice came out low, icy, and controlled—even when I was anything but.

His gaze flicked to mine, that wolfish grin never faltering. "Just making an observation, sweetheart."

A copper tang spread across my tongue as I bit down hard, using the pain to anchor me, to keep me from lunging at him right then and there. "Let me make one too," I said, my voice ice-cold. "It's funny how you've got so much time to run your mouth when you should probably worry about your game.

Wouldn't want the coaches to start wondering if you're too distracted to keep your roster spot."

The smirk slipped just a little.

"I don't care what you say about me," I continued. "But keep running your mouth about Mav, and we'll have a problem."

Craig's eyes narrowed, but someone's voice cut through the tension before he could say anything.

"What's going on here?" Mav growled.

I turned just as he stepped around the corner, his eyes flicking between Craig and me. His eyes darkened, looking dangerous, like he was seconds from dropping his gloves. His jaw was tight, tension radiating off him in palpable waves. It seeped into my chest, tightening my lungs as his gaze pinned Craig like a predator sizing up prey. He looked at Craig like he was one wrong word from slamming him through the drywall.

Craig chuckled, pushing off the wall. "Nothing, Davis. Just a friendly chat."

Mav didn't buy it for a second. He stepped closer, his voice low and deadly. "You sure about that?"

Craig held up his hands, feigning innocence. "Relax, man. Just making conversation."

Mav's gaze stayed locked on him, unyielding. "Then I'd suggest you find someone else to talk to."

Craig hesitated. A beat of silence stretched uncomfortably, but he must have seen something in Mav's expression that made him think twice. With one last smirk in my direction, he turned and strolled down the hall, the other guys wisely going with him.

The moment he was gone, Mav turned to me, his expression unreadable. "You okay?"

I nodded quickly. "Yeah. It's nothing."

His eyes lingered on mine, stormy and unspoken. He looked like he wanted to say something, to rip through the wall of hurt and half-truths between us, but didn't know where to start. He felt ready to demand answers and peel away the barriers I'd built until nothing was left between us. But after a long moment, he exhaled, running a hand through his hair.

"Come on," he said. "Where were you going? I'll walk with you."

I didn't argue. I tipped my chin toward the players' lounge, where Vivi and Selene were waiting, my heart thudding loud enough to drown out my doubt. As we walked, I couldn't shake the feeling that things between us weren't just complicated—they were a fuse burning toward an inevitable explosion. And I wasn't sure which terrified me more: the fire or the fact that I didn't want to run from it.

Later that night, shrouded in the darkness of my apartment, as the weight of silence finally settled over me, I curled into a ball on my mattress, my thoughts spinning—my fight with Mav, the confession, the way he looked at me like I'd betrayed him. I couldn't blame him for feeling that way. But I also couldn't forget the way he touched me after—like the betrayal didn't matter as much as the fact that I was still there, like we were tangled in something too real to be ignored.

I wasn't sure what scared me more—losing the job, or losing him. Because now I knew. That night in Vegas hadn't just been meaningless sex. And it wasn't a mistake the second time either.

I told him I would wait to get the annulment to protect his future, and I meant it. But that wasn't the only reason I hadn't pushed to get the paperwork done. *The truth?* I hadn't wanted to let go of it. Of him. Not yet. Maybe not ever. And that realization lodged deep in my chest like a secret I wasn't ready to face out loud. Especially after he called me *wife*.

CHAPTER EIGHTEEN

MAV

Two days had passed since I'd found out about our marriage, and I couldn't stop thinking about Nyx—my *wife*. The word was still foreign on my tongue, scraping against the inside of my skull every time I thought about it. I should've been furious. I should've called a lawyer and maybe even started the process of wiping the slate clean. But I wasn't, and I hadn't. And that scared the hell out of me.

That night in Vegas hadn't stayed in Vegas—it had followed me home and tangled itself into my life like a barbed wire threading through my ribs so I couldn't unravel. And when I thought about it... *why would I?* Whenever I considered letting it go, it seemed like ripping that thread free would take pieces of me with it.

My phone buzzed, and when I saw the name on the screen, it felt like the universe had read my mind—my best friend, Skye— the one person I could talk to. Relief shot through my chest. I answered immediately. "Hey, Skye. How did you know I needed to talk?" If anyone could talk me off this ledge, it was her.

"My Spidey senses were tingling."

Her daughter, Lily, chattered in the background, and as her voice rose in a high-pitched squeal, Skye's laugh followed.

"She's rearranging my pantry and stacking cans like they're Legos. It's chaos over here."

I grinned at the picture she painted. "Sounds like my kind of fun."

"Seriously, though, is everything okay? Is it your dad?"

"No, it's not about Dad. He's... still fighting. Keeps telling me not to worry, but it's hard not to when I'm here and they're back home dealing with everything."

"I'm sorry, Mav. I'm here if you need to talk. Or need anything at all."

"I know. Thanks." I leaned my head back against the worn leather headrest of my SUV. I still had fifteen minutes until I had to be inside the arena for practice. I'd half contemplated calling Skye as I sat in the parking lot, debating about going in early. My fingers had been drumming against the steering wheel, restless, like they couldn't decide between flight or fight. "Remember the rookie Vegas trip? The team-building thing before camp started?"

"Yeah, where you hooked up with a Margot Robbie look-alike for a night to remember? Such a player."

Her teasing jab sent a jolt of guilt swirling in my gut. "That's the one. And you better not have told Liam. You're my best friend—confidentiality is part of the job." I tried for a laugh, but it sounded thin even to my ears.

"I know. I kept that detail to myself." Her voice softened, and I could imagine the small smile curving her lips. She knew exactly how wrecked I was without me saying it. "I've got your back, just like you've always had mine."

"I miss Lily. You guys need to come to California and visit when you're able." I'd carried Skye's secret like it was my own, just like she would carry mine now.

"She misses you too. Now stop stalling and tell me what's going on."

I told her what happened when Coach insisted I have an assistant, one whom I hadn't recognized from the drunken haze I'd been in the first time we'd met. We'd grown to be friends, or at least, our working relationship was easy, and I trusted her—or I had until finding the marriage license.

"Wait. Married? As in legally-tied-till-death-do-you-part married?" She didn't wait for me to answer, words rolling out of her mouth quickly. "And I love her name, by the way. Also, why didn't she tell you?"

"She said she was figuring out how to get it annulled then just dove into working for me and let it slide." The words tasted bitter.

"I bet she did. She's got a hot hockey husband. And since you've consummated the marriage—twice, including Vegas…"

My blood heated at the memory. "Yeah." My hand curled in my lap like it still carried her imprint. I missed the feel of Nyx's silky skin, wanted to hear the sounds she made when I touched her, needed to feel the desperation and passion of her response all over again. "That's the thing. It was good. Too good. It wasn't just a random hookup—I can't stop thinking about her. About what it felt like… being with her. She got under my skin, and I don't know how to get her out." And maybe I wanted that imprint to stay, proof that she'd reached me when no one else could.

"What, she wrecked you for anyone else?"

Yeah, she did. I wouldn't say it aloud, but Skye's comment hit home.

She muffled the phone to answer Lily. "Sorry, she wanted a snack. But seriously, I'm not making fun of you." Honesty rang clear in her voice. "Liam did the same for me. You know how he messed with my head when I walked away freshman year. Is it like that? That feeling of 'I can't live without her,' just like I had with Liam, no matter how determined I was to try?"

There was no bullshitting Skye. My chest burned from holding the truth too tight. Skye and my sister had been best friends. We'd lived next door to each other, and after my sister died, Skye and I had formed a sibling relationship that'd only grown with time. I trusted her with my life, and she'd trusted me with her biggest secret.

"I don't know. I'm torn up about the situation."

"You don't think she targeted you, right?"

I could hear the worry in her question. "At first, yeah." I wanted to believe the worst. It would've been easier.

"And now?"

"It doesn't make sense. Why work as my assistant if she could've cashed in by selling our story with proof of the marriage license? And I don't buy the bullshit Ellis is spreading about her being a jersey chaser looking for a husband to bankroll her future."

"That asshat? You've already told me enough about him that I wouldn't listen to anything that came out of his mouth. He sort of reminds me of your cousin."

My cousin was a piece of work and had stirred up more shit with the football team than was healthy. He'd also sparked a fight between Liam and me during our first year in college.

"Besides, if you're probably going to replace Ellis as a starter, then of course he's out for blood." Skye was quiet for a moment then sighed softly. "So, what are you going to do?"

"I don't know," I admitted, dragging a hand over my jaw. "Part of me wants to shake some damn answers out of her. Just grab her shoulders and demand to know why the hell she let it go this far. The other half of me wants to sit next to her on the couch again and pretend everything's normal."

"You could... start with a conversation that isn't laced with accusations," she offered gently. "Just talk to her, Mav. I mean, really talk to her. It's obvious you care."

I rested my head against the seat and stared up at the headliner. "I'm worried I'll ask questions I don't want answers to. I don't know a lot about her life, not really."

"You already have the answers," she said softly.

I flinched, her comment hitting me harder than expected.

"You just haven't decided if you're ready to believe them. As for learning about her, that's something you'll have to work on. She'll open up if she has the same mindset as you."

I didn't respond right away. The truth was an arrow in my side—embedded too deep to ignore but too sharp to pull out clean. And if I tried, I wasn't sure I would survive the blood loss.

"I should go," I said finally, spotting players through my windshield as they trickled into the arena. "Practice starts in ten."

"Hey, Mav?"

"Yeah?"

She hesitated. "Whatever happens... don't shut her out completely, okay? You're not the only one who might be scared."

My throat tightened. "Yeah. I got it."

"I'll tell Lily you said hi."

"Tell her I miss her." I paused. "And thanks, Skye."

"Always."

I hung up, tucked the phone into my pocket, and stared at the arena entrance. I exhaled slowly, squaring my shoulders—time to stop avoiding the storm. And walk straight into it.

The locker room was buzzing with conversation. I tried to lock in on the murmurs drifting my way, but all I heard was static until I caught my name. Nyx's name. Then, Ellis's voice, low and as smug as ever. The sound of it was like a match to kindling.

"Davis better watch his back," he said just loud enough to

carry. "Wouldn't be surprised if he ends up the next Jennings. Mark my words—girls like her? Always come with fallout."

There was a beat of silence, then Craig added, "She's Trina's stepsister, you know. I know her past. Let's just say her rep isn't as squeaky-clean as she pretends."

Muted laughter followed—uneasy, the kind of forced laughter that didn't reach the eyes and died too quickly. I clenched my jaw, gripping the edge of the bench until my knuckles turned white. The air felt heavier, the walls a little tighter.

"Cut the crap, Ellis," St. James muttered, not needing to yell, his tone as sharp as steel. "She's done nothing to warrant your misguided interest. Stop feeding rumors. You don't even know her."

"Don't I? She's my fiancée's stepsister," Ellis shot back, a knowing smirk twisting his mouth. "Nyx was in Vegas, right? You wouldn't believe the level of manipulation she used to get this job. And now she's here, living the dream, glued to Davis's side like she belongs. It reeks of the relationship she had in college—the guy headed to the NBA that she dumped when he had a career-ending injury. You really think her being in Vegas, or ending up as Davis's assistant, is a coincidence?"

My vision tunneled. *Vegas.* The word hit me like a fist to the gut. None of the other bullshit he'd said registered. Ellis didn't know anything. He couldn't. But the way he said it, the way he twisted things—it made my stomach churn.

I stood abruptly, my discarded gear scraping against the floor. The conversation around us died instantly.

Ellis glanced at me, something flickering beneath his arrogance, something like satisfaction. He'd been fishing for a reaction, and I'd just given it to him.

I clenched my jaw. "If you've got something to say about Nyx, say it to me." Because no one talked about her like that.

Logan Reeves shifted uncomfortably but didn't speak. Tim

Shaw crossed his arms as his gaze flicked between us like he was debating whether to step in.

Ellis lifted his hands in mock innocence. "Relax, Davis. Just making an observation."

I took a step forward, lowering my voice. "Yeah? Here's an observation for you—keep her name out of your fucking mouth."

For a second, I thought he might push back. But then he did what he always did—he smirked, taking the coward's way out. "Touchy."

Then he made the mistake of bumping my shoulder as he passed. It was slight. Maybe even accidental. But at that moment, it was all I needed. My fist collided with his jaw before I even realized I'd swung. Pain shot across my knuckles, but it wasn't enough. It only made me want to hit him again.

Ellis stumbled back, eyes flashing with something between fury and delight—because, of course, he wanted this. He wanted the fight. He'd been waiting for it just as much as I had.

I barely got in another shot before St. James grabbed my arm, yanking me back.

"Enough!" The authority in his voice cracked like a whip. "Davis, stand down."

West was there a second later, stepping between Ellis and me, shoving Craig back against the lockers.

"You wanna run your mouth? Fine," West snapped, broad enforcer shoulders braced like a wall I didn't want to run into as he glared at Ellis. "But you're not screwing with this team just because you've got a personal vendetta. Davis isn't Jennings. Just because Nyx works for him doesn't mean he's pulling the same shit."

Ellis wiped the blood at the corner of his mouth, his cocky smirk returning. "That's cute. You're all lining up to defend Davis now?"

St. James shook his head, his grip still firm on my arm as he made damn sure I wasn't about to go for round two. "No, we're just done with your bullshit."

Ellis's expression flickered—just for a second. Because he realized he was standing alone. Logan Reeves and Ethan Mercer —his usual crew—weren't stepping in. They weren't backing him up this time. Tim Shaw kept his arms crossed, expression unreadable, but he wasn't taking Ellis's side either.

Ellis snarled, grabbing his gear. "This team's soft."

Funny, he was the one bleeding.

Hayes, watching from the bench lining the room, let out a low chuckle. "Nah, man," he said easily. "This team's just done with your ways."

Ellis's smirk faltered.

Hayes shook his head, leaning against his locker, stretching his arms. "Might wanna start packing your shit, Ellis. You keep stirrin' the pot, and your days here could be numbered."

Ellis didn't respond. He slung his bag over his shoulder and stalked out of the locker room. I was glad to see him go, even if it wasn't over. Not yet. Silence settled over the space, but the tension had shifted. I exhaled, shaking out my fists, willing myself to cool off.

St. James released his hold on my arm but shot me a warning look. "You need to stop letting him get under your skin."

I rolled my shoulders, still buzzing with adrenaline. "I'm working on it."

West clapped me on the back as he passed. "You should've hit him harder."

I huffed out a laugh. "Believe me, I wanted to."

Hayes's voice carried from the bench, his tone easy but knowing. "Doesn't matter. He's digging his own grave."

I met his gaze and believed him. A few minutes later, I got the summons to Coach's office.

Craig was already there, slouched on the bench outside like he didn't give a damn. Blood had crusted beneath one nostril, and one of his knuckles was split open. He didn't look at me when I walked up. He didn't have to. The tension between us was molten and festering.

The assistant coach poked his head out. "Ellis. You're up."

Craig pushed off the bench, shoulder checking me as he walked past. I clenched my jaw but stayed still. Just like I had in the locker room and before I'd finally snapped.

The office door closed behind him. Muffled voices rose immediately. I bet Coach didn't even wait for Craig to sit. The walls weren't thick enough to block out the fury.

"You think throwing punches in the locker room makes you a leader?" There was a slight pause. "We've got sponsors who will walk at the first hint of drama or media alerts. Keep pulling this crap, and you'll be off the ice before playoffs. The league's already on edge after last year. You want to be the next Jennings headline? Because that's how it happens." Coach's voice escalated even more. "Your ego isn't worth our brand. And it sure as hell isn't worth this team's season."

I shifted, arms folded, the sting of those words crawling up my spine. They weren't wrong. I'd been on the receiving end of Craig's bullshit for long enough. But hearing how close it all was to unraveling hit differently when it wasn't coming from him. It was coming from the people in charge.

The door jerked open. Craig stormed out, jaw tight as he avoided eye contact.

"Davis. Sit," Coach barked from behind his desk.

I stepped in, shut the door, and sat.

"You let him bait you," Coach said, not mincing words. "You want to prove you're more mature than Ellis? Then act like it."

I stayed quiet, tension coiling low in my gut.

Coach leaned back, arms crossed. "You're one of our strongest players this season, but you don't get a pass. That kind of outburst gives the media a narrative. It gives the league a reason to question what we're building here."

"I wasn't trying to start something," I said, voice low. "But I'm not gonna keep letting him take swings without taking one back."

Coach's expression didn't budge. "Then stop giving him opportunities to get under your skin." He exhaled hard, like this entire conversation was one long migraine. "Look, the last thing we need is another PR nightmare. You're not Jennings, but people are watching. And they're not going to wait for the facts before they start drawing conclusions."

I nodded once. "Understood."

Coach studied me. "I need you focused. Not distracted by fights. Not by press. And definitely not by drama off the ice. Can you do that?"

The question was more loaded than it sounded. I met his eyes. "Yeah. I can."

"Then prove it. Starting now."

I stood, my chest was tight, my fists looser than before, but the heat under my skin hadn't cooled. Not fully. I would take the hit, take it and redirect it, because he was right about one thing—I didn't get a pass.

I left the office with the echoes of both lectures ringing in my ears. Craig might've lit the fuse, but I'd been holding the match. And now, I had to figure out how to keep it from blowing up everything else.

CHAPTER NINETEEN

NYX

I tried to focus on my laptop, but my attention drifted to the ice. Craig was at it again. A familiar dread coiled in my stomach. My fingers hovered over the keys, frozen as my gaze slipped back to where the guys practiced. Every drill, shift, and play, he found some way to get under Mav's skin. And with each shove, it was as if my ribs caved a little more, invisible hands squeezing harder with every play. A shoulder clip here, an extra-hard check there. It was subtle enough to stay inside what was acceptable, but I saw it. So did the coaches. And so did Mav. With every dirty play, his restraint was slipping.

I tightened my grip on my laptop, my stomach twisting. The edges of the computer dug into my palms, grounding me against my spiraling thoughts. The plexiglass in front of me blurred, my laptop forgotten. I blinked, trying to clear the fog creeping into my vision. Craig circled Mav like a vulture would fresh prey, waiting for the moment Mav's patience snapped. It was going to boil over. Before my anxiety found a stronghold, a voice pulled me back.

"You're thinking too hard," Vivi Rhodes teased, a playful sharpness in her eyes as she slid into the seat beside me. She leaned in and bumped my shoulder with hers, a knowing grin curving her lips as she handed me a water bottle.

I accepted it, grateful for the distraction.

Selene St. James perched next to her, arms crossed. "I can see the smoke coming out of your ears."

It almost made me smile. "I can't help it," I admitted. *How could I not get dragged into Craig's orbit when Mav was right there?*

"We noticed," Selene said dryly. "You're always working, always watching."

I laughed. "Pretty sure that's literally my job." But this felt less like work and more like survival.

"Yeah, yeah." Vivi waved a dismissive hand, her expression softening. "But even assistants are allowed to breathe. And lucky for you, we're here to be a distraction."

"Oh?" I arched a brow. "What's the distraction?"

Selene grinned. "Charity gala."

I blinked, and my heart stumbled a beat, momentarily pulling me from the brewing disaster on the ice. "What?" The single word escaped, blank and automatic, my brain slow to catch up.

"The annual team gala," Vivi clarified, shifting to face me. "You're coming. No excuses."

I hesitated, struggling to find an excuse for why she would be looking at me like that. "I don't think that's my place." A shadow of doubt crept in.

Selene scoffed. "You practically run Mav's life. If anyone deserves a ticket, it's you. And we need you there. Trust me."

"Besides," Vivi added with a sly grin, "you don't want to miss watching Mav suffer through wearing a suit."

That pulled a small laugh out of me. "I can't picture him in one." The mental image alone stirred an unwanted curl of heat low in my stomach. But I could picture a lot of other things on Mav—or off him—too easily. I hated that he could still twist my insides into knots with a single thought.

"That's because it happens exactly once a year and only because the guys have no choice." Selene smirked. "But apparently, Mav hasn't complained about it, unlike some of the guys."

Vivi shot me a knowing look. "Wonder why that is."

Heat crept up my neck. "Don't start." Because if they did, I wasn't sure I would have the strength to stop them. Or keep from confiding in them.

"What? We're just saying—he's different around you compared to how he is with everyone else. Our husbands even mentioned it." Vivi's tone was casual, but her gaze was sharp, cutting through my defenses like a blade dressed in velvet. "Less distant. Fewer get-out-of-my-way vibes. More... whatever that was." She nodded toward the ice.

I followed her gaze just in time to see Mav glance up—directly at me. My breath caught, stalled in my chest. Our eyes met for half a second, his smoldering, reminding me of what he'd looked like last night. Heat bloomed beneath my skin as memories of tangled limbs and gasped names crashed through me. It felt like a thread snapped between us, fragile and electrified, and it wasn't until he turned back to the drill that my lungs fully expanded again.

Selene let out a dramatic sigh. "Wow. Riveting. The tension is unbearable."

I rolled my eyes. "You two are ridiculous." I couldn't deny it to myself. The tension wasn't just unbearable. It was suffocating.

"We know." Vivi grinned, elbowing me. "But you like us anyway."

I didn't argue. God help me, I really did.

"So, it's settled." Selene flicked her long, curly hair over her shoulder. "You're going. End of discussion."

A protest scratched at the back of my throat but never made it out as Craig's name-calling reached my ears. I froze.

"You're a puppet, Davis," Craig taunted. "Stepsister or not,

Trina had to pull some serious strings for her. Bet Nyx thinks you're her golden ticket."

My stomach knotted, and a chill danced down my spine. Vivi's eyes narrowed.

"Don't," I softly warned because I didn't trust myself not to lose it.

"Oh, I won't," Vivi replied. "But he's an idiot. Everyone can see it."

The seats in the stands were cold, but I barely felt them. My laptop sat open on my knees, emails organized neatly on the screen, but I hadn't typed a word in the last fifteen minutes. My focus wasn't on my work. It was on the ice. On Mav. And on Craig, who was circling him like a predator waiting for the right moment to pounce.

I wasn't a hockey expert, but even I could see what was happening. And it was about to blow wide open. The way Craig slashed his stick a little too close to Mav's skates and hit a little harder during drills was always right on the edge of legal. It wasn't just competition. It was personal. And I hated that I was fuel for the fire.

Mav, for his part, was trying to ignore it. Each tight line of his body was a warning flare. He was laser focused, his movements sharp and controlled, but every time Craig came near him, I saw the flicker of tension in his shoulders. He was holding back, but I didn't know how long that restraint would last. Part of me wanted him to unleash his fury on Craig.

I glanced around the arena. Most of the coaching staff watched with their arms crossed, clearly aware that something was brewing but not stepping in. The zero-tolerance policy from the media scrutiny they'd been under after Jennings's upheaval last year had made everyone hesitant to call things out unless they absolutely had to. My stomach churned. This was going to boil over—soon—and when it did, there would be no going back.

Craig swept past Mav, his stick jabbing just enough to disrupt Mav's balance. My spine stiffened, helpless fury burning at the base of my throat. Mav recovered quickly, but I caught the sharp glare he shot in Craig's direction. The next time they collided, it wasn't just a brush but a deliberate shove. Craig shot backward, skates slicing into the ice as he barely kept himself upright.

The whistle blew sharply. "Knock it off!" Assistant Coach McCabe barked. He stood near the boards, arms crossed, chewing gum like it had personally offended him.

Mav didn't respond, his chest rising and falling as he stared Craig down. Craig, of course, smirked like he'd gotten what he wanted. He skated up beside Mav, voice low enough that I couldn't hear—but I saw the way Mav's jaw clenched, the muscles in his forearms tightening around his stick.

I closed my laptop, already preparing for the inevitable.

Then it happened. Craig rammed into Mav harder than necessary. Mav's stick clattered to the ice as he spun, shoving Craig back with enough force that he nearly lost his footing. The moment Craig found his balance again, he dropped his gloves. So did Mav. They collided, fists flying, the sharp crack of impact echoing through the arena. The sound jolted through my spine. The bench erupted with shouts, players either calling for them to break it up or egging it on. Skaters stormed the ice, whistles blaring as they tried to pull them apart.

I rose from my seat, heart in my throat.

Vivi grabbed my arm. "Let them handle it," she murmured, but my chest burned as I watched.

Mav landed another solid punch before they were finally separated, breathing hard, eyes locked in a silent war.

"Get to the locker room, both of you!" the coach snapped, fury dripping from every word. "Now!"

Mav wiped his mouth with the back of his hand, barely sparing the coach a glance as he skated toward the exit. Craig followed, throwing me a smug look as he passed by the stands. My stomach twisted. Nausea curled low in my belly, sour and bitter, as the reality of Craig's game clicked into place.

I wasn't sure what Craig's endgame was, but one thing was clear—he wasn't done making my life hell. And I had a sinking feeling that Mav had just given him exactly what he wanted.

CHAPTER TWENTY

MAV

Reds and purples painted the sky as the sun sank below the horizon. My mind still swirled with the news I'd learned about Nyx and me two days ago. I barely made it ten steps into the parking lot before she caught up with me, her face flushed with frustration. The second I saw her, my blood fired hotter—not from the fight, from wanting her.

"You didn't have to do that," she snapped.

Her sharpness cut straight through the adrenaline still pulsing in my veins. I turned, my patience wearing thin. "Do what?" I knew what she meant, but I needed her to say it.

She huffed, crossing her arms. "Jump in like I can't handle Craig myself."

Her words scraped against every protective instinct I had. They sandpapered over raw nerves, exposing every jagged edge I'd tried to keep buried. I ran a hand through my hair, the tension from the locker room still coiling tight in my chest. "You shouldn't have to handle him at all." Not while I was around.

Her jaw clenched. "I've been dealing with guys like him my whole life, Mav. I don't need you to fight my battles."

Her rejection was a slap to my already-bruised pride, but I caught a flicker of something else beneath the fire in her eyes. She was lying—to me and maybe to herself. The way she said it—like I was making things worse and she didn't need me—made something snap inside me.

"Yeah?" I took a step closer, and the air between us tightened. I lowered my voice. "Why does it piss you off so much when I have your back?"

Her breath hitched, and for a second, neither of us moved. The parking lot was empty around us, the cool air pressing in, but I barely felt it—because all I felt was her.

Her glare flickered, something warring behind her eyes. "I don't want you to feel like you have to."

I exhaled sharply, the frustration and heat twisting into something else entirely—something dangerous, inevitable. She didn't get it. I *wanted* to. "Nyx..." But before I could stop myself, before I could think—I kissed her. Hard. Desperate. Unplanned.

My hands found her waist, fingers splaying like I could hold her together when everything else was falling apart. Her breath caught, her fingers curling into my jacket. For a split second, she kissed me back—just as desperate, just as wrecked. Then, just as fast, she pulled away. We both froze.

The absence of her mouth was like the air being sucked from my lungs.

Her lips parted, and her chest rose and fell too fast. I could still taste her, still feel the imprint of her against me, and I knew from last night that I'd just crossed a line we couldn't uncross. And I didn't want to.

Her eyes searched mine, wide with something unreadable—hope, fear, regret. I saw it all tangled in her gaze; maybe the same chaos was tearing me up inside. Then, without a word, she turned and walked away. My body swayed toward her, instinct before common sense, but I let her go. Holding her would've meant surrounding her with something neither of us was ready for, and I had no idea what the hell I was doing. At least, I tried to tell myself that. It didn't work because one thing was clear—I wasn't finished with her. Not even close.

The air still buzzed from the fight, from the kiss, from everything we weren't saying. Nyx turned away from me, her shoulders stiff as she crossed the parking lot. But I wasn't ready to let her go—not yet, not like this. I caught up to her in a few long strides, heat still thrumming beneath my skin.

"Nyx," I called out, low and rough.

She stopped but didn't turn around. Her spine was too straight, too tense, like she was holding herself together with fraying thread. "Don't," she said softly. Not sharp, not biting—just tired, worn down to her bones.

But I couldn't leave it there. I wouldn't. She looked wrecked, and not just from the fight. From me. And I hated that I couldn't take that part back.

"Tell me why Craig keeps going after you," I pressed, stepping closer until only inches separated us. The chill in the air didn't touch me, not when she was so close. "It's more than just how you got your job, isn't it?"

She sucked in a breath, and for a second, I thought she might shut me out completely. But then she slowly turned. Exhaustion cast her eyes in shadows, but beneath it, something raw flickered—like trust on the edge of shattering.

"It's because of Trina," she admitted, voice barely above a whisper. "Craig... he's her fiancé. And Trina is my stepsister."

Her words slammed into me like a body check. "She's your what?"

The memory of Craig's smugness flashed behind my eyes—the way he'd looked at her like she was already his to toy with. My jaw clenched. *Of all the guys on the team who would have a personal connection to her, it had to be him.* Then I remembered his recent comment about really knowing Nyx because she was his fiancée's stepsister.

Nyx let out a bitter, humorless laugh that held years of buried hurt. "My dad married her mother. Trina and her mom mostly hid their animosity toward me until he passed away. Then, all bets were off. I became a complication neither of them wanted."

Pieces slid into place like jagged glass—Nyx's hesitation, her walls, Craig's venom, Trina's cold disdain.

"I don't want to get into it any more than that. We have some family issues. Hopefully, Craig will back off soon. But"—she placed her palm against my chest for a too-brief heartbeat—"if he doesn't and he keeps interfering with you on the ice, I'll say something to Trina. I'll make it stop."

"I—"

"Mav, please." Her gorgeous eyes were misted with unshed tears, gutting me more than a punch ever could. "I'm sorry. I am. But please just let it go. I don't have the energy to get into everything. Family is family. Sometimes, they do shitty things to the people they're related to."

I understood that more than I cared to admit. Exhaustion rolled off her in waves, and I did the only thing that felt right. I gave her space. But I wasn't giving up.

From this argument, I would not stand down to Craig. If he wanted to be a bully and drag her name through the mud, he would always find my fist in his face.

CHAPTER TWENTY-ONE

MAV

The energy inside the arena was electric, a live wire buzzing just beneath my skin. But it wasn't just the game or the crowd that had me wired. It was Nyx short-circuiting every thought in my head. The look in her eyes when I kissed her, how she pulled away as if I'd scorched her like I was danger she couldn't risk, and maybe I was. It still crawled under my skin, fusing with the adrenaline pumping through me. Every time I blinked, I saw her eyes, stormy and furious, lit with something I didn't want to name. *And under all that?* The memory of her mouth on mine, like a brand.

The crowd's roar echoed through the tunnels as I tightened the laces on my skates, their bite steadying. I rolled my shoulders to shake off the nerves. This wasn't my first time in a packed stadium, but tonight was different. I was the starting right forward—Ellis's spot. Coach had shifted him to the left. He was still starting, but by his expression, the change hadn't sat well with him.

I kept my head down, forcing my breath to slow as I mentally traced the familiar pattern of my routine. It kept me grounded. If I let my thoughts drift to Nyx, to that kiss, to the chaos brewing off the ice, I would lose the edge I needed to survive this game. I could feel the weight of Ellis's stare from across the locker room. He didn't need to say anything—not yet. His posture—the way he sat hunched, elbows resting on his knees, jaw tight—was all the confirmation I needed. He hated this, hated me. Not because of anything I'd done personally but because I was in the spot he thought belonged to him.

A sharp snap echoed as he broke a hockey stick over his knee. The sound was like a gunshot, sharp and jarring, ricocheting straight through my chest. The crack of wood splintering made a few of the guys glance over, but no one said anything.

Ellis just leaned forward, voice low. "Don't fuck up, Davis."

His words hit like a slap, but it wasn't fear twisting my stomach. It was fury—controlled, coiled tight in my chest, just waiting for the right moment to strike. I didn't even blink. Didn't flinch. Just let the tension stretch between us until it was taut enough to snap. Then, with deliberate ease, I reached for my stick, tested the flex, and gave him a slow smirk. "Wouldn't dream of it." I forced a slow, cocky grin, letting the fire simmer behind my eyes. Let him see it. I wouldn't back down and wanted him to feel every ounce of my conviction.

His nostrils flared, but Kieran St. James clapped me on the back before he could say anything else. "Let's go, rookie. Time to prove why you belong here."

I pushed to my feet, rolling my shoulders as I followed my team from the locker room. Ellis stayed and didn't immediately rise to head onto the ice. I could feel the frustration rolling off him in waves, but I didn't care. I was done playing his games.

The crowd's screams thundered in my ears as we lined up. The roar swallowed my thoughts, but under it, my mind drifted —Nyx's voice, how she'd challenged me in the parking lot, and how she'd kissed me back like she hated herself for it.

The game was about to start. The puck hit the ice, and

instinct took over. The tension in my chest unraveled, replaced with sharp focus. The game moved fast, bodies colliding, skates slicing across the ice as we fought for possession.

I cut through the neutral zone, tracking the play, my pulse steady. The puck bounced off the boards, Rhodes catching it clean before sending it my way—or so I thought.

Ellis intercepted it in mid-pass, deliberately cutting off the play. My jaw clenched so tight I thought my molars might crack. That bastard wasn't just undermining me. He was trying to make me fail in front of everyone. In front of her, where it would sting the most. It wasn't just a bad read. It was deliberate.

I skated hard to recover. Ellis sent the puck off wildly, a turnover that gave the other team a prime scoring opportunity. Our goalie saved it, but St. James's voice was sharp when we headed to the bench.

"Play like that again, Ellis, and you won't like the ice time you get next period."

Ellis didn't respond, but the look he shot me was venomous. I exhaled slowly, keeping my composure as both teams left the ice before the start of the second period.

It wasn't long before the Zamboni finished resurfacing the ice and we reentered the rink, then the next period was officially underway. We were up two to one when it happened. I was moving into position when I felt a shift in the energy on the ice. It was the kind I couldn't always see, but I could feel it.

Ellis didn't attack me directly. Instead, he set me up.

A hard check sent me into the boards—not from him but from the other team's enforcer, a guy I'd barely exchanged words with. *But the way he grinned down at me as I caught my breath? And how he glanced past me toward Ellis?* It clicked. Ellis had conveyed to the guy that I wasn't protected and was fair game.

I clenched my jaw, shoving off the boards, skating back into the play. Fine. If Ellis wanted to throw me to the wolves, I would make him regret it. I wasn't just playing for my place on the team anymore. I was playing for something bigger—someone with stormy blue-green eyes and a spine of steel who deserved more than a front-row seat to my downfall.

The puck was dumped into our zone, and Ellis had a chance to clear it out. I was open. I tapped my stick, calling for it.

He looked at me. Then passed it straight to an opposing forward.

They scored seconds later.

St. James slammed the boards with his stick, frustration rolling off him in waves. "Ellis! What the hell was that?"

Ellis's expression was unreadable, but he skated back toward the bench like nothing had happened. I forced my breathing to stay even. It wasn't a mistake. It was sabotage. And I wasn't about to let him get away with it.

We filed off the ice for intermission. Coach barked orders while we caught our breath. The third period began in no time, and we stormed back into the rink.

Tied game. Two minutes left. I was tired, sweat dripping down my back as I lined up for the face-off. The ref dropped the puck, and I exploded forward, muscling past my opponent to gain possession.

Ellis was on the ice, and he didn't outright ignore me.

I caught the puck clean, skating toward the net, waiting for the hit that didn't come. Instead, Ellis was shadowing me, forcing me into a bad angle—boxing me in so the other team's defense could lay me out. If Ellis thought I would let him box me in, he didn't know me. I'd spent my whole damn life fighting out of tight corners.

Instead of letting him control the play, I cut hard, dumping the puck back to West. He sent it cross-ice to Rhodes, who lined up the perfect shot. For a beat, the world held its breath, then the puck slammed into the back corner of the net. Rhodes pumped his fist and skated backward a wide grin plastered on his face.

The arena erupted. The horn blared, strobe lights flashing white-hot over the ice as the crowd surged to its feet in a thunderous roar. My teammates crashed into me, shouting, gloves slapping helmets, arms locking around shoulders.

But it wasn't the victory that roared in my chest. It was defiance—raw, unfiltered, and louder than the thousands of voices around me. This wasn't over. Not by a long shot. I turned, expecting to see Ellis sulking. Instead, he was skating straight for me. His stick raised like he was celebrating—except his eyes were burning.

I didn't move as he skated past, voice low. "Enjoy it while it lasts, rookie."

I wanted to tell him he was right. I was enjoying it. My gaze momentarily flicked to where Nyx sat, on a high from shutting Ellis down and proving to myself and everyone watching—especially her—that I was meant to be here. But belonging on the ice meant nothing if I didn't figure out where I fit with her.

Instead of rising to Ellis's bait, I gave a smile as sharp as a blade. "You too." And I meant every word.

Because the way St. James, West, and Rhodes pulled me into a huddle seconds later was proof of what Ellis refused to admit. I was part of this team. And he was on the way out.

CHAPTER TWENTY-TWO

NYX

Numbers blurred together on my computer screen, bleeding into one another like my shaky focus, as dizzying as my thoughts and twice as disorienting. Sleep had been a stranger. Food an afterthought. *And Mav?* He was an ache that refused to fade, buried so deep it felt like it had wrapped around my ribs. My fingers trembled against the keys, vision tunneling as I tried to focus, but my body had long since given up on me. I was running on fumes, every breath too shallow, every blink too slow.

Mav had been distant since we'd slept together four days ago. The uncomfortable space between us gnawed at my already-frayed nerves. *Did he regret it? See me as the mistake I always feared I was?*

I'd freaked out, desperate for things to return to how they'd been before he'd found out about our Vegas marriage. There was also the possibility that his change in attitude didn't fully have to do with me. Maybe it was the weight of his dad's illness or Craig's chaotic and dangerous behavior on the ice.

Or it was me. Maybe he saw through the desperation beneath my carefully constructed façade. *What if he hates me for it?* That possibility alone sent ice through my veins. I caught him studying me sometimes. His gaze felt like a touch—hot, searching, peeling back my layers until I was raw and bleeding beneath it. Every look was a warning bell, a silent countdown to the inevitable crash.

The more time I spent around him, the more the past clawed at the edges of my resolve. How he moved, how he laughed with his teammates, how his eyes softened when he talked about hockey—it was dangerous because I remembered him like that, before everything, before I'd exposed our future with the Vegas secret I'd buried so deep, I prayed it would never surface. I couldn't let myself fall into that with reckless abandon because trust had led me straight to this precipice once before. And this time, the fall to my heart would be fatal.

A low hum of conversation filtered through the open conference room door, catching my attention. I wasn't trying to listen, but my name in Craig's mouth was enough to still my fingers over the keyboard.

"Davis is going to crash and burn," Craig said with a laugh that set my teeth on edge. "He's letting his elevation to professional-athlete status go to his head with that smokin' hot assistant. Mark my words. He'll fall off his rookie pedestal just like Jennings."

A few chuckles followed, but they weren't unanimous.

"She looks like hell lately, but that doesn't take away from how hot she is." Craig's voice was too casual to be innocent.

My pulse spiked, my teeth grinding until my jaw ached. Bastard. He didn't care about facts, only wreckage.

"Wouldn't be surprised if she's on something. Probably popping pills to keep up with Davis's schedule. Hell, maybe they're both using. That would explain a lot, wouldn't it? The way they look half dead most of the time."

That one hit like a sucker punch hollowing out my chest until there was no breath left to steal. He wasn't just coming for me anymore. He was going after Mav by using me as leverage. A smear campaign dressed up as locker-room banter. *And the worst part?* It wasn't even about me. Craig's position on the team was slipping, and he knew it. Going after Mav was his power play. I was just the weapon in his hand.

But the strings? I knew exactly who was pulling them—Trina. I could feel her presence in the cruel precision of the words designed to humiliate. Craig was being fed lines, whispered to behind closed doors, reminding him how to twist the knife.

The old, familiar helplessness surged, curling cold fingers around my spine. No matter how far I ran, Trina always knew how to tighten the noose—her grip invisible but suffocating. My hands curled into fists, fingernails biting into my palms as I forced myself to stay silent, when all I wanted to do was scream.

"Jesus, man," someone muttered. "You're reaching."

"That's enough, Craig." I recognized Zane West's voice, sharp and edged with warning.

Nick Hayes followed up with a steely command. "If you've got a real concern, take it to Coach. Otherwise, shut your damn mouth."

A tense silence followed.

Craig laughed, a hollow sound. "Whatever. I'm just calling it as I see it."

A few guys chuckled, and someone else chimed in—Ethan Mercer, if I had to guess. "You think she's actually into him or just, you know, doing her job?"

My stomach twisted, the implication hitting harder than it should have. Because part of me wondered the same damn thing. *Am I just doing my job? Or am I hopelessly tangled in this marriage I'm too afraid to want?*

"Does it matter?" Craig replied. "Girls like that always have an angle. Give it a few months, and she'll be on to the next one after whatever scandal she brings hits the tabloids."

A beat of silence followed before Zane's voice cut through,

sharp and unimpressed. "Maybe shut the hell up, Craig. You sound obsessed."

Nick followed up, calm and firm. "Yeah, man. You got a thing for Davis or something? You talk about him more than anyone else does."

Laughter rippled through the group, this time not at my expense.

Craig scoffed. "Just saying. I've been around long enough to know how this works. She's Trina's stepsister, and my girl talks. That alone tells me everything I need to know."

I clenched my jaw, willing myself to breathe through the fury burning beneath my skin. At least Zane and Nick weren't buying into his crap. Small mercies. It wasn't much, but it was something. And right now, I clung to scraps of hope like a lifeline.

My phone buzzed, snapping me out of my thoughts—a calendar reminder for a PR meeting with Harper. I stood, my legs stiff, my head pounding, and made my way toward the other wing of the facility. As I passed through the staff corridor, a few glances followed me, some curious, some unkind—no doubt Trina's handiwork, her whispers weaving poison wherever they landed.

When I reached Harper's office, her door was already open.

She didn't look up from her screen. "You're five minutes late. Sit."

I obeyed, trying to smooth the wrinkles from my skirt as I sat. Harper Reynolds, the team's PR strategist, had a reputation that preceded her. Not a hair out of place, or a single crease in her suit. Harper could have been carved from glass and ambition. Sharp as a tack, she had zero tolerance for bullshit. We'd already met during onboarding, but she rarely called for one-on-ones with assistants.

Her hazel eyes finally rose to mine. "There's chatter in the locker room, on the ice, and it's not good."

I swallowed. My stomach hollowed, fear clawing along my throat. I'd known this was coming, but hearing it felt like a guillotine blade suspended over my neck. "Okay..."

"Word is there's tension surrounding Davis and you."

My pulse stuttered. "I haven't done anything."

Harper leaned back in her chair, lacing her fingers together. "That's why I wanted to talk one-on-one. Because perception can become reality if we don't get ahead of it. I've got sponsors watching the team, higher-ups asking questions, and a locker room that doesn't need another scandal."

I sat straighter. "I haven't had any issues with Mav or Craig. Not directly."

"Not directly." Her brow rose. "Interesting, though, as I didn't mention Craig."

I hesitated. I fell into that one too easily. Damn it. One slip, and I'd given away too much. My past always had sharp edges, and I'd just cut myself on them. But walking past Trina's handiwork while going through the staff room had put me on the defensive. The problem was I didn't know how much I could tell Harper.

I studied the no-nonsense brunette sitting across from me. She wasn't much older than me but had immense responsibility and was respected and feared by the guys on the team. But I wasn't on the team. I was a new hire, and with that said, I doubted she, or anyone else, would go to bat for me, since Trina and Craig would have seniority.

Instead, I gave enough information to get her off my back but not enough to reveal the entire situation between Trina and myself. "Craig's implied some things around others. I've kept my head down and stayed professional. But he's... persistent."

Harper nodded like she'd expected it. "That's all the information you have for me?"

I clenched my trembling hands in my lap. My nails dug crescents into my palms, a silent reminder to hold it together just a little longer. "I can't think of anything else that's relevant." It wasn't a lie. Not really. The problem was a family one that should not impact my working relationship with anyone else. Trina I couldn't control, unfortunately.

A few seconds passed while Harper studied me then seemed to take me at my word. "I'm going to have a conversation with Mav then with Craig. I just wanted to hear your side first."

I nodded tightly, uncomfortable with how much I was keeping from her—the marriage, my stepsister's hatred. If I was lucky, none of it would come out and Harper wouldn't have to head up the nightmare that would follow.

"I appreciate that."

"Look, Nyx," she said, her voice softening slightly, "you're walking a tightrope, whether it's fair or not."

I was so damn tired of tightropes, of balancing acts that left me breathless and bruised from the inside out.

"I'm not here to judge what's going on behind the scenes, but I am here to keep this team from falling apart. If things escalate —if the situation between Craig, Mav, and you becomes a distraction—I will have no choice but to make recommendations."

"I understand."

She stood, signaling that the meeting was over. "Get some rest. And drink some water—you look like you're about to pass out."

The words turned out to be prophetic. It was like Harper had peeled back my armor and seen the fractures beneath the surface. I couldn't keep pretending I was unbreakable. I barely cleared her office door before the world tilted. My vision blurred, and I stumbled as I grabbed for the edge of a filing cabinet—but missed. A sharp cry left my lips. The world spun, the fluorescent lights blurring into a kaleidoscope. My knees buckled, the cold floor rushing up to meet me as darkness swallowed everything whole, hungry and absolute.

CHAPTER TWENTY-THREE

MAV

Nyx had collapsed, and I found out too damn late. By the time Harper called me, Nyx was already in the back of an ambulance, disappearing from the arena like a nightmare I couldn't wake from, no matter how hard I clawed at the edges of it.

I'd driven to the hospital on autopilot, struggling to see through the haze of frustration and the gnawing pit hollowing my gut. The lobby smelled like antiseptic and bitter coffee. The sharp scent clung to my clothes and skin as I stalked down the hall, my jaw clenched tight.

I stopped at the nurse's station, my pulse hammering in my throat. "Nyx Lawson. She was just brought in."

A few nurses glanced over, one looking vaguely familiar, but I couldn't place her. My focus shifted to the one with short black hair, who glanced at a computer screen then at me.

"And you are?"

"Maverick Davis. Her husband," I ground out.

Her expression softened, surprise flashing across her features as she flagged down an approaching doctor with bushy white hair and eyebrows. He looked more like a mad scientist than a doctor.

"Doctor Westley, this is Maverick Davis," she said quickly. "He's Nyx Lawson's husband."

"Caught the game the other night—hell of a play you made in the third period."

I gave a distracted nod and mumbled my thanks.

He read my expression and offered a tight, professional smile. "Well, it's a good thing you're here, Mr. Davis." The doctor leaned against the desk beside me. "Your wife's lucky, but she's been pushing herself too hard in her condition."

His words barely registered. "Her condition?" The words clipped out of me, sharper than intended.

The doctor's gaze softened like he thought he was delivering good news. "She's pregnant. Severe exhaustion and dehydration, likely compounded by early pregnancy fatigue. She needs rest and proper care." He paused, glancing at the chart. "You caught this early. She and the baby will be fine if she slows down and stays hydrated."

Pregnant. The word exploded in my head, echoing louder than the crowd at a playoff game. The floor rocked beneath me. Blood roared in my ears. It wasn't just shock. My chest cracked open as if I'd been waiting for this truth without knowing it.

My mind spun, my dad's fight mixing with what the doc had just told me about Nyx. Dad had been slipping more lately. I hadn't told Nyx how bad it had gotten, how the last call had ended with him forgetting I'd even been drafted. Mom tried to soften the blow, but I heard it in her voice—the fear, the help-lessness. *And now?* I had someone else I could lose. The parallel to how Liam, Lily's dad, hadn't been in her life from the start slammed into me. *Would Nyx tell me, or cut me out?* The weight of it all hit at once.

"I'll head in to speak with her once she's fully awake," the doctor added. "She was still sleeping when I checked earlier.

We're giving her fluids, and I'm prescribing a prenatal vitamin. You're welcome to go see her, but give her a moment to come around."

I must've responded with something appropriate. My legs carried me without permission, my mind stuck on a loop of that single, shattering word. I arrived at her room on autopilot, in a daze from the life-altering news the doctor had revealed. Pregnant. I was still processing.

Silently, I opened the door to Nyx's room then stopped short at the sight before me. I didn't know what I expected to find when I finally saw her, but it wasn't this. Not her looking so... breakable. Her gorgeous ocean eyes were closed, and dark lashes fanned against skin so pale it made something inside me twist painfully.

The blankets were tucked around her, and her dark hair was spread over the pillow, but they did nothing to hide the dark half-moons beneath her eyes or how pale she was. Worn to the bone, like life itself had been siphoned out of her while I wasn't looking. I pushed the feeling down. Hard. I hated seeing her like this more than I could admit.

Movement by her bed drew my attention. I only had eyes for her and hadn't even noticed the nurse who adjusted the drip to Nyx's IV. The nurse's assessing gaze landed on me.

"Are you family?" Her dark eyes narrowed. Her question echoed of routine with a hint of challenge.

My throat worked around a sharp and unwieldy knot. "Yes." I hesitated, pulse thudding in my ears. "I'm her husband." If claiming her kept me close enough to protect her, I would say it as often as I had to.

At the edge of my vision, Nyx stirred. Her lashes fluttered against her pale cheeks, a crease forming between her brows.

"Mav...?" Her voice rasped, rough with confusion. Then her eyes snapped open, the tail end of my conversation registering in her expressive gaze.

My body felt like it was underwater, heavy, limbs refusing to cooperate, a dull ache pulsing behind my eyes. I met her gaze head-on, daring her to deny what I'd said. Daring her to reject me or to tell me I didn't belong at her side when everything in me rebelled at the thought. Her full lips pressed in a tight line, and we held our silence until the nurse left the room. The click of the door felt deafening, sealing us in with too many words unsaid and not enough air between us.

I exhaled slowly, dragging a hand through my hair. This wasn't right. None of it. She'd been hiding something from me —I'd known that. But looking at her now, her skin too pale under the fluorescent lights, there was more to her exhaustion, way more. After the doctor's news, it all made sense. I couldn't help but wonder if she'd known.

"Mav?" Her voice, hoarse and scratchy, yanked my gaze back to her. She blinked at me, confusion and something like disbelief tightening her features. "You told them you're my husband?"

My jaw flexed. "I am, aren't I? Or was that just some drunken joke to you?" The sting of betrayal and panic gnawed at me. *If I hadn't been here to hear it from the doctor himself, would she have told me?* The thought clawed at my chest. It felt a little too similar to what Skye and Liam had gone through.

She flinched, her fingers curling tighter around the hospital blanket. "You didn't have to say it."

I barked out a hollow laugh, stepping close to her bed. I despised how empty it sounded, hated more the crack of fear behind my irritation. I couldn't untangle the twist in my chest. *Was it anger at her or myself for not seeing this coming?* "Forgive me for using the one damn fact I know about us." My voice sounded rough, bitter. "Unless you would prefer I stand here as nothing to you." Even as the words left my mouth, they burned. I didn't want to be nothing to her.

Her lips parted like she wanted to argue, but they pressed

back into a tight line. Her gaze skittered away from mine. "I didn't ask you to be here, Mav."

The crack in my chest widened. "Yeah? Well, someone has to be, Nyx. Because with what's going on, you clearly can't handle it alone." She shouldn't have to.

I was being terrible, and even though I knew it, I couldn't stop myself. Flashbacks of my best friend doing this alone—and also not telling the father—tore through my mind. I didn't like the similarities, not one bit.

Her breathing hitched, and something broke behind her eyes—barely there, gone in a blink. She shut it down fast, pulling that practiced indifference over her like armor. "Just go," she whispered, but her voice splintered on the last word.

My jaw flexed. One step—that was all it would've taken to close the distance between us. My fingers twitched at my sides like they were waiting for permission to reach for her, to do something, anything, to ground her. But I didn't move. Didn't breathe.

I forced myself to stand there, every muscle strung tight, frustration twisting under my skin with something heavier I didn't have a name for. "I'm not going anywhere." And this time, I meant it—in every way that counted.

CHAPTER TWENTY-FOUR

NYX

Tension radiated off Mav like a force field, crackling in the air between us. He crossed his arms over his chest, clenching his jaw tight, his expression carved from stone, unforgiving and unreadable. His presence filled the room, heavy and suffocating, like the walls were shrinking inward. I swallowed hard, but the knot in my throat wouldn't budge. It only tightened with all the things I couldn't say.

Tears stung my eyes, but I refused to let them fall. I couldn't. Not now. Not in front of him. If I cried, it would feel too much like surrender, confirmation of every ugly thing spinning between us, every fear that I was weak, a mistake he regretted.

He didn't move. He didn't argue or leave. He stood his ground like a marble-carved sentinel, and his gaze locked on me as if I were the battlefield and the war all at once. I hated how it twisted something vulnerable inside me—because part of me didn't want him to leave. Part of me needed him to stay, even if I didn't know what I would do with him if he did.

A knock at the door broke the suffocating silence, and the doctor entered. His face was calm, but there was a spark of good humor in his eyes as he glanced between us. The doctor's easy expression scraped against my nerves. "Ms. Lawson—or should I say Mrs. Davis?" he asked, and the title hit me like a slap, rendering me mute, before he addressed Mav. "And Mr. Davis."

The formal words reminded me of everything tangled between us—names that didn't feel real but bound us just the same.

"I've reviewed your test results. We've already spoken briefly." His eyes flicked to Mav with professional ease. "But I wanted to go over them together."

My pulse pounded in my ears as I sat up straighter, fighting the dizzy wave that crested over me. It was just my luck that the doctor had talked to Mav. I never should have put his name on the HIPPA paperwork. It was a moment of weakness when I realized I had no one but myself. It was something I now regretted. "What is it?" My heart thundered against my ribs, every beat like a warning drum in my chest.

"The primary cause of your collapse was severe exhaustion and dehydration," he explained. "But there's another factor we discovered." He offered a small, congratulatory smile. "You're pregnant."

The word resonated between us like an explosion, obliterating whatever shaky ground I thought we stood on. The room spun, a sickening spiral that dragged me under. My fingers dug into the blanket, the fabric bunching in my palms. The walls swam in my periphery, the air thick and syrupy, clinging to my throat like it wanted to choke me, impossible to draw into my lungs.

"Are you sure?" My voice cracked on the question. Raw and scraping desperation bloomed, as if saying the words might rewrite them.

"Positive," he confirmed, his tone gentle but firm. "The lab confirmed it, even though you're early on. We'll schedule a follow-up appointment and provide you with a proper care plan. Rest, hydration, and avoiding stress are top priorities."

His words blurred together, a list of instructions I couldn't process—because all I could hear was that one word, echoing, relentless.

He left us alone with the bombshell still ricocheting in my chest, the echoes rattling through my mind. The door clicked shut, sealing us in like a tomb. Silence swallowed the room whole. My chest squeezed tight, and my breath caught between denial and panic. *Pregnant.* The word clawed at my ribs, refusing to be ignored. It thrashed inside me, wild and frantic, as if my heartbeat had turned against me. The word didn't just echo. It took root. Every cell in my body seemed to revolt and rejoice at the same time.

No wonder Mav was so angry. He must've thought I knew— or that I would keep it from him like I had the knowledge about our marriage.

I risked a glance at him, half expecting him to bolt, to run from the wreckage between us, but he didn't move. He stood there, looking at me like I was the only thing tethering him to the floor. The silence stretched thick and oppressive, pressing down until I thought it might crush me. It made something fragile in my chest twist painfully, because I didn't know if that weight would steady him—or drag us both under.

"You didn't know?" Surprise rippled through his voice.

My eyes filled with tears I refused to shed. I shook my head.

Mav moved closer, slow and deliberate, his gaze steady. "We'll figure this out."

My throat was tight, almost too tight to speak. "You don't have to say that."

"I'm not saying it because I have to." His tone gentled. "I'm saying it because I mean it."

His words wrapped around me, dangerous and warm, a lifeline I wasn't sure I could reach. When I finally forced my gaze to meet his again, I saw something in his eyes that almost undid me—determination, resolve. But deeper than that, fear—and hope. It scared me more than anything, that spark of belief. Because part of me wanted to reach for it, even knowing how badly it could burn.

For a breathless moment, I wanted to believe him. I wanted it so badly it hurt. *But trust?* My remaining family had taught me to be wary. Trust was a luxury I no longer knew how to afford.

CHAPTER TWENTY-FIVE

MAV

I kept glancing at Nyx as I drove to her apartment, my knuckles tight around the steering wheel, tension radiating through every muscle in my arms. She hadn't said much since we left the hospital, and every quiet mile felt like a weight settling deeper into my chest.

Her eyes were shadowed, her lips pressed together as if she was holding herself together by sheer force of will. I could see her trying to fold in on herself, to disappear into the passenger seat. But there was no way in hell I would let that happen.

We pulled up in front of her building, and I killed the engine, letting the silence hang for a beat longer. "You sure you're okay to go up?" I asked, my voice rougher than I intended.

She gave a tight nod but didn't move to open the door.

"Nyx."

Her gaze flicked to mine, and I saw the cracks in her armor for a second. Exhaustion. Fear. Something deeper, heavier, laced with resignation and maybe something dangerously close to defeat.

"Come on," I said, gentler this time. I got out, came around to her side, and opened the passenger door. She hesitated then let me help her out.

Her steps were slow, careful. I kept my hand on her lower back as we climbed the narrow staircase to her unit. She fumbled with her keys, her fingers trembling, and I took them from her without a word, slid the key into the lock, and turned. The door swung open, and the first thing that hit me was how empty it felt—how sparse the furniture was. The space seemed hollow, stripped of comfort. Like it had never really been a home.

Then my gaze snagged on the paper held to her fridge door with a magnet. Red ink screamed from across the room—Final Notice. Eviction. A sharp pulse fired through my chest. I stepped forward and snatched the paper from the fridge without waiting for permission. The date stamped across the top gutted me.

"Nyx," I said quietly, holding it up. "You're getting evicted?" The words tasted like ash in my mouth.

She swallowed, her shoulders stiffening. "I was. It doesn't matter now." Her voice was flat.

"The hell it doesn't." Heat flared under my skin. "Why didn't you say anything? Why didn't you tell me things were this bad?"

"Because it wasn't your problem. I was handling it."

But she wasn't. And I had been too blind to see it.

"I—I thought I could keep my head above water." Worry threaded her too-quiet voice. "This job will keep me here. I'll be able to pay more of the back rent, and I'll be current… soon."

I exhaled hard, pacing a few steps before turning back to her. Not that I needed further proof, but this was it. "If all you cared about was money, you would've sold our story weeks ago. Hell, you could've sold it the day you took the job. You could've blackmailed me, gone to the media—"

"That's not who I am," she bit out.

"I know," I said, calmer this time. Because fuck, I did. The truth of it slammed into me, all the pieces falling into place. She'd never used the marriage. She'd buried it like it was a scar, not a weapon. She'd hidden it so deep, it had to be cutting her from the inside out, while she was working herself into the ground, trying to prove she could do the job without strings attached. And I had no doubt that when she could come up for air, she would've found some way to get the marriage annulled without the press or anyone else catching wind of what we'd done in Vegas.

I dragged a hand through my hair then sat heavily on the edge of her worn couch. "Tell me everything. The full story about Trina. Ellis. All of it." My voice came rougher than I meant, but I needed her to lay it all bare—no more half-truths between us.

Nyx stayed frozen for a beat then crossed the room and sank onto an armchair diagonally from me. She looked down at her hands, twisting them in her lap, then she took a shaky breath. She released it like she was emptying years of poison from her lungs. "I've already told you Trina's my stepsister and Craig's her fiancé. But it's more than that."

I stayed silent and let her find her words.

"When my dad got sick, I dropped everything. My boyfriend at the time had suffered a career-ending injury—or, at least, I think it was. He'd planned to go into the NBA, had a promising future. It was around the time Trina and Craig started dating, so they knew him. But my life imploded and Dean, my boyfriend, didn't understand why I couldn't be there for him. Things ended on bad terms. He's not really an issue, but Trina and Craig like to remind me I bailed on him. I ran, just like I tend to do."

She took a deep breath, and I held mine, waiting for what else would come.

"My dad was all I could think of. So I broke up with Dean, and I left college, moved back home to take care of my dad. I thought it would be temporary." Her voice cracked, and she swallowed hard. "But it dragged on. I didn't find out until after he'd passed, about a year and a half ago. Cynthia, my stepmother, had somehow convinced my dad to change his will. She ended up with it all. The trust, the house. I don't even know how. Dad would never have left me with nothing."

My fists clenched in my lap.

"She uses me for appearances, keeps me close enough to parade around my father's friends when it suits her because they're influential, but behind closed doors? I'm nothing." Her mouth twisted, like the taste of the truth soured on her tongue.

She pressed her hands together so tightly her knuckles turned white. "I tried to go back to school, but the debt crushed me, since I had no job prospects. Cynthia and Trina didn't lift a finger. Worse, they pushed me into their events like I was some prop for their perfect life." Her gaze rose to mine, her expression raw. "The Titans assistant position… It was the one chance I had to benefit off Trina because she needed me to do something for her. I-I was able to push back for once, get a job I desperately needed."

"You fought for it," I said softly.

She nodded, something like pride flickering for the first time. "Yeah. I did."

My chest twisted, tight and burning. "You do know you're nothing like them."

Her breath caught.

"Nyx, I haven't been able to get you out of my head. Not since Vegas." Not since she crashed into my life and set it all on fire.

She hesitated, teeth sinking into her bottom lip, her expression vulnerable but brave.

"It wasn't just sex," I pushed, rough and true. "Not for me. Both times… they meant something. They still do."

Her eyes glistened. Then she reached for me, her fingertips brushing mine, and it felt like the first breath after drowning.

"They meant something to me, too," she whispered.

Relief crashed through me, messy and all-consuming. "We're going to do this together." I closed my hand around hers. *Nyx and the baby are worth it.* "We'll figure out the marriage, the baby. There's no going back. Not for me."

Her hand tightened around mine, not much, but it was all I needed. Since the doctor's words had shattered my world, I could finally breathe. The weight in my chest didn't disappear, but it shifted because we were carrying it together. *And that?* That changed everything. It was like anchoring a lifeline—hers to mine, mine to hers.

But just as fast as relief settled, the storm creeping in around the edges of my mind roared back to life, because this wasn't over. Not by a long shot. Ellis and Trina wouldn't let this go quietly. They would come at her first, just like they always had. That was done. I wouldn't let her fight that battle alone.

CHAPTER TWENTY-SIX

NYX

Mav and I agreed to work things out. We were taking it slow. Meaning I stayed in my apartment last night, winning one battle and circumventing the one he didn't even know about—how I still didn't have electricity. I told myself it didn't matter. Candles and battery-powered lanterns were enough. Honestly, I'd lived through worse. But some part of me still felt like I was hiding the truth, not to protect him—but to protect myself from what accepting help might mean.

I would have power soon. Payday was around the corner, and things would be okay financially. Somehow. That didn't mean I would accept help from Mav. I was doing this on my own. I wanted it that way.

At least, that was what I kept telling myself. With the baby, that was different, but it was so new, and I didn't want to think too far into the future. The word felt foreign, like a coat that didn't quite fit but was already too heavy to shrug off.

I rested my hand briefly over my still-flat stomach, needing the connection. It didn't take long, only a second or two, for me to fall in love with the little peanut growing inside me.

I stifled a yawn as I walked into the arena in midmorning. I knew something was wrong the moment I stepped inside and too many eyes whipped to my face. The air snapped taut—charged, electric with the kind of tension that only came from ugly rumors or a scandal breaking wide open. Conversations hushed as I passed, eyes flicking toward me before quickly looking away.

My phone had been buzzing nonstop since this morning, but I hadn't checked it. I didn't have to. The whispers, the stolen glances, and how even the staff avoided my eyes told me everything I needed to know. Somehow, the news of my hospital stay and the baby had leaked. And I bet I knew just which ER nurse had done that.

I swallowed hard, keeping my head high as I approached the offices. My heart pounded, but I forced my steps to stay steady. If I looked rattled, letting them see even a flicker of fear would only make things worse.

"You've got to be kidding me." Trina's sharp voice cut through the hallway, dripping honey and venom in equal parts. Her arms crossed as she stood outside one of the conference rooms, looking at her phone. She lifted her gaze just as I walked past, and her lips curled in satisfaction. "Oh, look who it is. The star of the show."

I didn't stop walking. "Not now, Trina."

"Oh, I think now is the perfect time." She fell into step beside me, her heels clicking loudly against the tile. "How did you pull this off? I have to admit, I'm impressed. It's one thing to land a cushy assistant gig, but to trap an NHL player in marriage? That's next level." Her smirk turned ugly, red mottling her cheeks as she hissed, "You have some nerve pulling this crap before *my* wedding."

The audacity of her entitlement made my stomach churn, but I didn't let her see it. I stopped so suddenly she nearly ran into me. My fists clenched at my sides as I turned to her, my tone low and biting. "You really think I planned this?" The tremor in my voice betrayed me. "That I wanted this?"

Trina's expression didn't shift. "I think you're a survivor, Nyx. You always find a way to land on your feet. And now, congratulations, you've just guaranteed yourself eighteen years of financial security."

The sheer audacity of her words sent a wave of nausea crashing over me, twisting my stomach so violently, I thought I might be sick. My fingernails dug into my palms as I fought for control. "You have no idea what you're talking about."

She arched a brow. "Don't I?"

Before I could say something I regretted, Mav snapped, "Back off." He stood at the end of the hall, his eyes locked on Trina, his jaw tight with barely contained fury.

Trina didn't even flinch. She just smirked, like she'd expected his exact reaction. "Oh, look. My stepbrother-in-law is here to save the day."

Mav ignored her completely, stepping closer to me. "Are you okay?"

I nodded, but it wasn't convincing because I wasn't okay. Not even close. Everyone knew our business, and I had no doubt that the missed phone calls this morning were Harper's demands we go to her office to handle the PR shitstorm that'd exploded from yesterday's hospital visit.

He exhaled sharply then turned back to Trina. "Stay out of this, Trina. Find someone else to mess with if you want to play games."

She lifted her hands, feigning innocence. "Relax, Davis. I'm just trying to understand how this all happened."

"Try minding your own damn business." Mav's voice dropped lower as his arm wrapped around my waist and pulled me into his side.

Annoyance flickered in Trina's gaze, but she recovered

quickly. With one last smirk, she turned on her heel and disappeared down the hallway. I let some of the tension seep out of my shoulders. Mav was still watching me, his expression unreadable.

"How bad is it?" I finally asked.

He hesitated, his pause saying more than his words ever could. "Bad."

My stomach lurched. "How did it even get out?"

Mav ran a hand through his hair, his frustration evident. "No idea. It could've been anyone. A hospital staff member, someone at the arena who overheard something—hell, maybe even Craig. But it doesn't matter. It's out now."

"Trina has a friend who's a nurse. I bet that's how the news spread." I rubbed my temples, exhaustion crashing into me. "I should quit."

Mav's head snapped up. "The hell you will."

I let out a humorless laugh, my phone pinging nonstop with alerts I'd set to Mav's name and mine. "Mav, look around. This isn't just some minor inconvenience. It's a media circus. I'm already the jersey-chasing gold digger in this story, and it will only get worse."

He took a step closer, his voice softer now. "You think running is the answer?"

I blinked up at him, my throat tight. "I don't know what the answer is."

His gaze searched mine, something unreadable flickering behind his eyes. "We'll figure it out—or I guess I should say, Harper will. We've been summoned."

Something in my chest loosened just slightly. But deep down, I knew this was only the beginning.

Harper's office door was unlocked, but she wasn't there. So we waited. It didn't take long for the team's PR liaison to storm in, her expression a mix of exhaustion and barely restrained irritation. Her heels were silent, unlike Trina's clicky parade. Harper didn't need volume to dominate a room.

"Sit," she ordered, not bothering with pleasantries, her door slamming behind her before she rounded her desk. Her tone brooked no argument.

Mav and I exchanged glances before sinking into the chairs across from her.

Harper tossed a folder onto the desk and crossed her arms. "Let's not waste time. You know why you're here." Then her gaze found me. "Pucking hell, Nyx. You should have told me."

Neither of us spoke. I pressed my lips together, a wave of remorse washing over me, as I managed a small nod acknowledging her reprimand. For as tough as Harper was, she was funny as hell, too, when she swore while using "puck" in inventive ways.

She exhaled sharply. "The news broke this morning, and it's spreading like wildfire. Reporters are already hounding the team for comments. I have at least four outlets trying to confirm whether or not our newly drafted star forward is about to become a father."

My stomach churned. I clenched my hands in my lap, willing myself to keep it together.

Mav leaned forward, his expression dark. "How the hell did this even get out?"

Harper shook her head. "Doesn't matter. It's out. And now we need to control the narrative before it spirals further."

I swallowed hard. "What... what are they saying?"

Harper flipped open the file and pulled out a few printed articles. "Speculation, mostly. Some are calling it a distraction for the team. Others are painting Nyx as a gold digger who targeted a rising NHL star. Then there's the power-play boss angle that's all yours, Mav." She slid one paper across the desk. The headline caught my breath: *Inside the Scandal: Is Maverick Davis's Assistant Carrying His Baby?*

I felt Mav stiffen beside me. His hands curled into fists against the armrests of his chair. "This is bullshit."

"Of course it is," Harper said flatly. "But it's the kind of bull-shit that can get out of control fast. So we need to get ahead of it."

I forced myself to look at her. "What do you need from us?"

Her eyes pinned me, as sharp as a scalpel. "Is it true? The marriage? The baby? Everything?"

Mav and I both answered. "Yes."

Harper's lips pressed together in a thin line before she turned to Mav. "And you're the father?"

I nodded, my voice soft but firm when I replied, "Yes."

Mav's jaw clenched. "Yes."

"I guess congratulations are in order." Harper sighed, rubbing her temples. "All right. Here's what's going to happen. We issue a simple statement—no drama, no unnecessary details. Something along the lines of 'This is a personal matter, and we ask for privacy while we navigate it.'"

Mav scoffed. "You think that'll shut them up?"

"No," Harper admitted. "It's too close to what happened with Jennings and interoffice power plays. But it'll give us time to figure out our next steps and paint a cleaner picture without fueling the fire."

She glanced at me. "Nyx, I won't sugarcoat this. Because of the speculation this team has been under for a prior player I don't need to name, the media will find whatever they can to spin this story into something scandalous. They'll dig into your past. Are you prepared for that?"

My stomach twisted. I had no deep, dark secrets, but I wasn't naïve. The moment reporters started connecting me to Trina and Craig, things would only get worse.

But what choice do I have? "I can handle it," I said, hoping that wasn't a lie.

Satisfied, Harper nodded. "All right. I'll draft the statement. In the meantime, keep your heads down. No public confrontations. No comments to the press. And for the love of God, no more fights with Craig."

She aimed the last part directly at Mav, who rolled his shoulders, defiance sparking in the tight press of his lips, but he didn't argue.

Harper gathered her papers and stood, irritation flashing in her eyes before it was gone. "I'll be in touch once we release the statement. Until then—stay quiet." She swept out of the office, leaving behind a silence that felt heavier than before.

I exhaled slowly, dragging a hand down my face, understanding her annoyance. I'd kept this from her. "This is a nightmare."

One second I was waking up in a hospital bed, and now? Now, my private life had been smeared across sports blogs and Twitter threads like blood in the water. I couldn't catch up—not to the headlines, not to the pitying looks, not to the tightening coil in my stomach every time someone said "congratulations" like it was a blessing instead of a time bomb. It felt like my life had cracked wide open in stages—first the fall, then the ambulance, and now this... the fallout I never wanted.

Mav turned to me, his expression unreadable. "It's only a nightmare if we let them win."

I wasn't sure what scared me more—the media, or that Mav had said "we."

After everything, I needed air. I needed space. But instead, I found myself in Mav's car, staring out the window as he drove. Neither of us spoke. I didn't know where we were going until the car slowed, the headlights washing over an empty parking lot. The crash of the waves reached me before I'd even registered we were at the beach.

I blinked as he parked near the entrance to the boardwalk and exited the car without a word.

When he realized I wasn't moving, he leaned down and opened my door himself. "Come on."

I should have argued. I should have said no. But my body moved on autopilot, walking next to him as the waves crashed against the shore. Salt-laden air blanketed my frazzled nerves, and the rhythmic rolling of the waves eased the tension inside me. It was peaceful. I paused, causing him to stop beside me.

"Why are we here?"

Mav exhaled, raking a hand through his hair before looking at me. "Because you needed to breathe."

I let out a shaky laugh. *How did he know to bring me here?* "And this was your solution?"

He didn't smile. "Yeah."

The weight of everything hit me all at once. The hospital. The rumors. Trina. Craig. The fact that my entire life had just been thrown under a microscope. My chest tightened, my throat burning.

Then Mav stepped closer. "It's okay." A cool, salty breeze swept in from the ocean, tangling my hair like it could undo the knots in my chest. His voice was quiet. Sure.

I shook my head. "No, it's not."

I don't know who moved first. Maybe it was me. Maybe it was him. Maybe it was both of us, drawn together like magnets set to collide. Suddenly, I was pressed against him, my fingers gripping his shirt, his arms around me, holding me tighter than he should have. I squeezed my eyes shut, swallowing past the lump in my throat. I shouldn't have let this happen. I shouldn't have needed him like this.

His hand slid up, his fingers brushing my jaw, tilting my face slightly. I felt his breath against my lips, its warmth sending a shiver down my spine. He hesitated. So close. Too close. But then he pulled back, his forehead pressing against mine for only a second before he stepped away completely. The air between us was thick and charged. But he didn't push. He didn't demand.

Instead, he whispered, "I've got you."

And I let myself believe him.

CHAPTER TWENTY-SEVEN

MAV

The next day, tension vibrated through me like a live wire. I was on the verge of exploding. Everywhere I turned, whispers followed. The rumors about Nyx and the power play of me being her boss had gone from murmurs to full-blown headlines overnight, fueled by Ellis's bullshit of tagging our story with Jennings's and the media's insatiable appetite for scandal. It wasn't just speculation anymore—it was a feeding frenzy. And I was done standing back while they tore her apart.

I was scheduled for a media appearance after practice. Harper was in on it and fully supportive. I made sure Nyx was watching from the sidelines, arms crossed, her face set in that unreadable expression she wore whenever she tried to protect herself from the world. Too bad she had no idea I'd already made up my mind about what I was going to do.

The second one of the reporters veered toward the topic, trying to frame Nyx as an opportunist, but I cut them off. "You want the truth?" I said, my voice steady and unshakable. "Nyx— *my wife.*" The words felt like a promise, a vow I wasn't ready to break. "Is one of the hardest-working people I know, and she doesn't deserve the bullshit rumors being spread about her."

The reporters exchanged glances, clearly caught off guard by my bluntness.

"She's been thrown into this mess because of me," I continued, my gaze sharp as it met the cameras. "So, if you want a scandal, talk about how the media loves to tear down a woman for daring to exist next to a pro athlete. Talk about how my personal life shouldn't be up for public consumption. But don't you dare come for Nyx like she's done something wrong."

Nyx's breath hitched from where she stood, but I didn't look at her. If I did, I might say something even more reckless.

Harper caught me before I cleared the cameras, her phone clenched in her tight grasp, eyes sharp beneath her professional calm. "Not bad, Davis," she said, her tone clipped. "You just bought us some time."

I blew out a breath. "Yeah? How much?"

"Enough to get ahead of it." She swiped her thumb across her phone's screen, pulling up her calendar. "We'll do some public appearances—low pressure, hand-holding, smiles, couple things. We make them fall for you two as a package. That's how we win this."

"So a charm offensive."

Her mouth curved, but it wasn't a smile. "No. We make them *believe* it's love."

I glanced toward where Nyx stood watching me. My chest tightened. *Love.* The word hit me hard because I'd been steadily falling for her for some time now. Because it wasn't pretend. Not to me. Not anymore.

The things I usually kept hidden, Nyx had never once thrown them back in my face. Then there were the nights we'd spent wrapped around each other, not just with heat but something calm and grounding that made everything else fade.

She'd suffered in silence more times than I could count and still managed to keep her head high and show kindness to others. Never once had she asked to be rescued or played the victim. She kept showing up with quiet resilience and fire behind her calm.

Then there was her smile—the one that crept in slow and lit up the whole damn room when it did. Her beauty was the kind that didn't need attention to be undeniable.

She never asked for anything. Never demanded the spotlight. Even when she had every reason to talk—and every weapon to use me—she didn't. She took care of things no one noticed, slipping into my life, handling matters, and never flinching at the chaos.

And the baby—she hadn't run from that either. What we had wasn't perfect. It was complicated, messy, real, but it was ours, and I wouldn't trade it for anything.

I glanced back to Harper. "That part's easy," I said quietly.

The weight of the cameras hadn't even cooled before I felt the fire building inside me again. Because no matter what Harper had spun for the media, one loose thread still waited to unravel everything—Ellis was gunning to have me traded. I'd already heard him talking with a reporter and making the connection, throwing me under the bus and stoking the story to a blaze.

The locker room was buzzing with post-practice chatter, the hum of conversation mixing with the clatter of gear being packed up. I stepped inside, my pulse thrumming with frustration, my jaw tight as I scanned the room.

Then I spotted Ellis lounging near his stall, acting as if he hadn't spent the last few weeks trying to turn the team against me. And like he wasn't responsible for half the bullshit swirling around Nyx's name. He was laughing at something Ethan Mercer had said, grinning like he didn't have a damn care in the world.

I saw red. I crossed the room in a few short strides, my body moving on instinct. Before I could stop myself, I shoved his shoulder hard enough to make him stumble back against the lockers. The chatter in the room cut off instantly.

Ellis straightened, rolling his shoulders, his smirk flickering just slightly. "What the hell's your problem, Davis?"

"You think this is funny?" My voice was low, as sharp as a blade. The fury bubbling beneath my skin felt like it might burn me alive. "Running your mouth, poisoning the team with your bullshit?"

Ellis scoffed. "Relax, man. It's just talk."

"Talk?" My laugh came out jagged. "You've been spreading lies about Nyx, about me, stirring the pot like this is some goddamn reality show." This wasn't about team politics anymore. This was about Nyx, about the family we hadn't planned for but I sure as hell would protect. "But I'm done playing."

He rolled his eyes, crossing his arms. "If she can't handle a little scrutiny, maybe she shouldn't be hanging around pro athletes."

My hands curled into fists at my sides, my body taut with restraint. "Let me make this crystal clear—you come near her, you so much as breathe another word about her, and you and I are going to have a much bigger problem than a few shitty rumors."

A commanding voice cut through the tension. "Enough," St. James snapped. The team captain stepped forward, his presence alone enough to make the room shift. His narrowed eyes locked on us both, but his focus landed on Ellis. "Ellis, you got something to say? Say it now. Otherwise, shut the hell up."

Ellis's jaw clenched, his smirk fading as he glanced around the room. His usual allies—Logan Reeves, Ethan Mercer, and Tim Shaw—weren't stepping in. They hesitated, exchanging uncertain glances as if suddenly realizing they were backing the wrong guy.

Mercer nudged Reeves with his elbow, lips twitching like he expected a show.

Rhodes stepped up beside me and grinned. His voice casual but firm, he said, "Yeah, Craig. What's the deal? You've been running your mouth like it's your damn job. Thought we were here to play hockey, not spread high school gossip."

Reeves stood back, arms crossed, his face unreadable. But he didn't laugh or back Ellis either. Shaw's mouth opened, but no words came out.

West leaned against his locker, nodding. "Seriously, man. You're making yourself look desperate." He cracked his knuckles, staring Ellis down without needing to say another word, the enforcer presence etched into his square jaw and steely gaze.

Ellis's lips pressed into a thin line, his shoulders tensing. He looked at me again, his eyes flashing with something unreadable before he scoffed and grabbed his bag. "Whatever," he muttered, shoving past me. "Like I said before, this team's gone soft."

"Also, like before, we're just done with your bullshit," Hayes called after him, his tone edged with finality as he didn't even look up from lacing his skates.

Ellis didn't look back. The silence in the room was thick as I exhaled, rolling out the tension in my shoulders.

St. James clapped a hand on my back as he passed by. "You handled that better than I expected." His voice was low, but the edge beneath it could've cut glass.

I let out a short laugh, shaking my head. "Believe me, it took everything in me not to do more."

"Yeah, well. I've heard from Coach." St. James smirked. "Let's just say his days here are numbered. Let him dig his own grave."

I nodded, the weight in my chest easing. Since this shitstorm had started, I knew I wasn't standing alone. But it was almost impossible not to throw the first punch, especially when Ellis was doing anything he could to set me up for the fall. The only reason I didn't hit him was because I was aware of who I would be facing when I walked through the door tonight—and she was worth more than a moment of losing control.

It took longer than I'd thought to finish up at the arena before heading home. When I pushed open the door to my condo, I wasn't sure what I expected. Maybe chaos, silence, or Nyx gone entirely.

What I didn't expect was to find her curled up on my couch, barefoot, wrapped in one of my sweatshirts that swallowed her whole. A throw blanket covered her lap, and an apple rested in her hand, half eaten. On the TV, a romantic comedy played— one of those cheesy ones with over-the-top confessions and improbable love stories. Something in its normalcy hit me square in the chest.

She looked... peaceful. But not in a fragile way—in a *real* way. Her gaze flicked toward me, and a small smile tugged at her full lips. Soft. Almost shy. But it was there. And damn if it didn't land straight in my gut.

"You're home late," she said, her voice a little rough from exhaustion but warmer than I deserved.

I shrugged out of my jacket and draped it over the arm of the chair. "Media circus ran overtime." We'd agreed on a modified work schedule for her. She needed rest, and I planned on making sure she got it. Many of the things she managed for me could be handled in the comfort of my condo, not requiring her to run herself ragged like she had been doing. *And groceries?* I made sure she set up a delivery service for that.

She arched a brow. "Did you survive without committing assault?"

"Barely," I answered, letting the corner of my mouth tug up. "Ellis is still breathing. But it was close."

A faint laugh escaped her. I watched her fingers twist around the apple, her knuckles pale. Maybe she wasn't as okay as she wanted me to believe. My chest pulled tight. After crossing the room, I sank onto the couch beside her. We were close enough that our knees brushed.

She didn't pull away. Instead, she let out a slow and shaky breath. "I guess Harper's prepping you for the next wave of damage control."

"Yeah." I ran a hand through my hair then let it fall between us, so that she could reach for it if she wanted to. "She's got a whole plan, which you know about. Public appearances, smiles, holding hands." I glanced at her. "Think you can stomach pretending you like me in public?"

Her smile turned real this time, a glimmer of that fire I'd always seen in her. "I think I can manage."

For a heartbeat, we just sat there. The TV played on, filling the quiet with ridiculous background noise, and the scent of apples drifted between us.

Then, softly, I asked, "Do you remember anything from that night in Vegas?"

Her smile faltered, something unspoken flickering across her face. She stared down at her apple like it held the answer. "Flashes," she admitted. "Laughing. Crashing another party with a terrible karaoke rendition of 'Summer Nights.'"

A rough laugh scraped my throat. "That was you?"

"Pretty sure it was you too."

"Damn." I shook my head, unable to fight the grin. "And the wedding? Anything?" Scattered flashes from the night had returned to me ever since I'd found the marriage license, but I wanted to hear what she remembered.

Her brows pulled together in thought. "A chapel with neon lights. An Elvis impersonator, or pastor, I guess, who smelled like whiskey and bad decisions. I remember looking at you and thinking..." Her voice trailed off like she was debating whether to say it.

I shifted closer. "What?"

Her eyes met mine, bare and brave. "Thinking, *This feels*

right. Like maybe, even in the middle of the worst idea of my life, you were the one thing that made sense."

My heart lodged in my throat. "Yeah," I rasped. "I remember that too."

Silence stretched, but it wasn't heavy. I could see it in her eyes—the moment she let her guard slip just enough for me to see beneath the layers. I reached into my pocket and pulled out the small velvet box I'd been carrying around like a weight against my ribs all day. Her gaze dropped to it, her lips parting slightly.

"Mav..." she whispered, her voice frayed at the edges. "Where did you—"

"I called in a favor," I said roughly. "St. James's jeweler. I told her I needed something fast. Described you, and she pulled this out without blinking."

I flipped the box open, the soft click loud in the quiet room. Nestled inside, the ring caught the light and scattered it like fire. The platinum band was sleek and strong, but there was more to it—an inlay of brilliant-cut diamonds traced the band in a subtle shimmer, and came with a matching wedding band. Not flashy, not loud. Just quiet strength. Timeless. *Her.*

The center stone was a two-carat diamond, not gaudy, not oversized, but cut so precisely it looked like it could carve glass. A perfect radiant, bold and unapologetic, the way she walked into every room like she belonged, even when she didn't believe it herself.

"The jeweler said the stone reminded her of someone fierce," I said, my voice low, catching her eyes. "Untamed. Beautiful without even trying. It felt like you the second she opened her safe." I paused, watching her stare at the ring like it was fragile and dangerous.

Her lips parted, then her breath shivered out. She didn't say a word. She didn't have to. Her throat bobbed as she swallowed, blinking fast. "I didn't think... I mean, with everything going on..."

"I didn't get it for the cameras." My voice was steady now, sure. "I got it for us. For *you*. So you'd know this wasn't just a situation we're surviving. It's something I want to build."

Carefully, I took her hand and slipped the ring onto her finger.

Her breath shuddered out as she stared down at it, the way it caught the light like a quiet promise. "It's perfect," she whispered.

"So are you," I murmured.

Her gaze flicked up, meeting mine. There was no hiding now—not her, not me.

Her apple rolled off her lap, forgotten as she reached for me. I met her halfway, our mouths colliding in a kiss that burned hot and deep. Her fingers tangled in my shirt, pulling me closer like she couldn't get enough.

I didn't fight it. I didn't want to. My hands found her hips then her waist, feeling the tremble beneath her skin. It wasn't desperation anymore. It was something more. Something real. Something ours.

Her lips parted with a quiet gasp, and I swallowed it down, kissing her harder, deeper. She pressed into me, the blanket slipping off her lap, forgotten.

"Bedroom," she breathed against my mouth.

I scooped her up without hesitation. Her laughter was breathless and soft in my ear as I carried her down the hall.

CHAPTER TWENTY-EIGHT

NYX

Mav's mouth was still on mine when my back hit the bed. The weight and heat from him lit a fire inside me.

He eased back just enough to look at me, his hand at the hem of my shirt. His thumb brushed the bare skin of my hip as he slowly pushed the fabric higher, lifting the sweatshirt inch by inch until it cleared my head. I shivered, not from cold but from how his eyes moved over me like he saw all of me. His lips parted, his gaze dragging down to where my lace panties clung to my hips. He swallowed hard, a growl catching in his throat.

I reached for him. "Mav..."

That was all it took. His mouth was on mine again—not rushed but reverent. He kissed me with purpose, with patience, as if this wasn't a mistake or a reaction to chaos but something he wanted, something real that belonged to both of us.

I tangled my fingers in his shirt, tugging him closer until he pulled away just long enough to drag it off. His skin was warm beneath my palms, muscles taut and flexing as I traced the lines of his chest and shoulders. He was solid and steady and mine.

He kissed down my neck, slow and aching, and my breath caught as his hand slid up my side. When his fingers hooked the edge of my panties and slid them down my legs, I didn't hesitate. I didn't overthink. I just felt—wanted, seen, *safe*.

He settled between my thighs, and I gasped at the first brush of his fingers. Gentle. Teasing. Building me until I arched off the bed, chasing the heat only he could give. My hips rocked up instinctively, a quiet cry escaping me when he pressed against my entrance. His breathing was uneven as he lined himself up, pausing.

"You okay?" he asked.

"Yes." I reached up and touched his face, my voice low but steady. "I want this. I want you."

He pushed in slowly, carefully, and the delicious stretch pulled a moan past my lips. I didn't tense. Not with him.

I felt everything, every inch, and when he stilled, letting me adjust, I wrapped my arms around his back and whispered, "Don't stop."

He buried his face in my neck, muttering something broken that sounded like my name. Then he shifted, and everything else fell away.

We moved together, breath for breath like our bodies had been waiting for this. Every thrust hit deep, building dizzying sensations that coursed through my body in fiery trails of heat. My legs wrapped around his waist, my fingers digging into his shoulders as he pushed me higher and higher until the world exploded behind my eyes. I shattered apart beneath him. He followed with a guttural moan and collapsed beside me, pulling me into his chest, still panting.

We lay tangled in the sheets, slick with sweat, skin to skin, his hand smoothing down my back in quiet, steady strokes.

I didn't need to speak, not yet. The silence between us held everything that mattered. The rhythm of his heartbeat beneath my cheek, the way his arms stayed locked around me like he had no intention of letting go—that said enough.

I wasn't bracing for impact. I wasn't waiting for the ground to give way beneath me. I was right where I belonged—held, seen, loved—and completely at peace.

I'd had enough. I'd let Craig and Trina drag my name through the mud for weeks. I'd taken every sly dig, every hushed whisper behind my back. I'd swallowed the embarrassment, shame, and exhaustion of constantly being on the defensive. Today was different. Mav had shown me what it was like to have someone stand by my side instead of against me, and something inside me clicked into place. He had my back. We were a team. And I was done swallowing my pride like it was survival. I wasn't going anywhere. And I sure as hell wasn't going down without a fight.

The entry corridor of the arena buzzed with early-morning noise—skates clattering in the distance, the faint hiss of the Zamboni prepping the ice, and voices drifting from the weight room, where I knew Mav was. But all of it faded as my gaze locked on them.

Craig leaned against the trophy case like he owned the damn place, arms crossed over his chest in that smug, arrogant way. Trina perched beside him like a queen overseeing her crumbling kingdom. Her glossy smile was all teeth and venom.

Not today. I strode toward them, purpose crackling in every step. "Hey, Craig."

His grin faltered just slightly, his shoulders drawing tight.

"Got a minute?"

Trina turned, arching a perfectly manicured brow. The overhead lights glinted off her statement two-carat diamond earrings like weapons. "Oh, look, it's the woman of the hour."

Craig chuckled, shoving his hands into his pockets like it was a game he was about to win. "What's up, sweetheart? Come to admit I was right, finally?"

A few staffers paused by the vending machine, conversations dying in mid-sentence. Behind them, a player in his team-issued joggers and hoodie glanced our way, his brows drawn tight. Even the maintenance guy froze beside his mop bucket, watching like he couldn't look away.

I folded my arms, leveling him with a glare. "Actually, I came to call you out for being the pathetic, manipulative piece of shit you are." I raised a brow, gearing up to drop a bomb Trina wouldn't like. "I'm curious, Trina, how long has it been since you spoke to Lara, because I doubt it's been that long for Craig."

Craig's smirk froze, just for a breath. Trina scoffed, but her gaze flicked to Craig, a split-second hesitation before she masked it with disdain.

"Excuse me?" she snapped, her voice thinner than usual.

I took a step closer, not backing down an inch. The cool draft from the arena entrance brushed against my neck, raising goose bumps beneath my shirt. "You've been spreading lies about me since the second I took this job. You've made it your mission to turn everyone against me. Why?"

Craig rolled his shoulders, but there was a tightness there, a flicker of tension in his jaw despite the lazy drawl. "Maybe because I don't trust women who magically show up in a guy's life at the perfect time, like when they go pro." He slung an arm around Trina's shoulders like she was his shield. "Or maybe it's because our rookie of the year married a damn staffer. A PR time bomb ready to explode."

Their game was obvious—her spite, his loyalty, their shared vendetta. I smiled, slowly and knowingly, as power twisted low in my gut. "Or maybe it's because you're terrified of Mav taking your spot on the ice."

His jaw flexed so hard I swore I could hear it crack.

"Bullshit."

"Oh yeah?" I crossed my arms tighter, my nails digging into my skin to keep my composure. I had another ace in the hole, but I wasn't planning on using it, not unless I had to. "Then why are you so obsessed with dragging him down?"

Trina sniffed, sensing an opportunity to twist the knife. "Oh please, Nyx. You act like an innocent victim, but let's be real—you've gotten good at playing the poor-orphan card."

My stomach twisted, bile rising, burning my throat, but I held my ground. No more flinching or backing down. I wasn't the same girl they used to push around. "And you excel at playing the mean girl, Trina. The only difference is that I stopped caring what you think long ago."

Her smirk faltered just enough for me to see the crack beneath the polish. Good.

Craig scoffed, shaking his head. "You really think Davis wants you? You're a scandal unfolding as we speak. And the league? Yeah, they're not gonna stand for it. Both of you will be out on your asses for the embarrassment you're causing the Titans."

I tilted my head, letting a slow, confident smile curl my lips. "I call bullshit. But I do have a question for you to ponder. Why is it that you're trying so hard to discredit me? And yet, no matter what you say, Mav stands by me. Or an even better question, why, despite your best efforts, are you losing control?"

Craig's nostrils flared. Trina's hawklike gaze bounced between us like she was finally seeing the cracks in her strategy.

"You've got some nerve," Craig growled, but the edge to his voice wasn't as confident as before.

I stepped closer until I could see the tightening of his throat, the flicker of panic he tried to mask. My voice dropped low, razor-sharp. "You've got a secret. One I'm sure Trina wouldn't love to find out about."

His face paled beneath his tan, his fists clenching. *Bingo.* I had him with that one. I'd never said anything to Trina when he'd basically attacked me late one night in the hallway of my dad's house. I'd endured a harsh, sloppy kiss and groping hands, but that was the extent of it because I'd threatened to scream and bring the house down with it as well as his engagement.

Trina's brow knitted, her lipstick-perfect mouth tugging into a slight frown. "What the hell is she talking about?"

That was for them to deal with. But I wasn't done. Not yet.

"You know what else I think?"

I turned fully to Craig, narrowing my gaze until it felt like I could cut through him. His smirk tried to make a comeback, lazy and careless, but it didn't reach his eyes.

"I think—no, I know—you're threatened by Mav, and it's been your game all along to feed any scandal around him so the league would be mad."

"Fuck that," Craig snapped too fast. "He's a rookie. He's got nothing on me. As for the scandal, he's doing that to himself."

I let out a slow, knowing hum, taking my time. "Then why are you so obsessed with him? Why do you care so damn much?"

A few more people had drifted to the edges of the corridor now, half hiding their curiosity. The weight of their attention made the air feel tight, like the entire arena was holding its breath.

"He's faster, smarter on the ice. His vision for plays? Next-level." I let the words hit their mark. "And you see the writing on the wall, don't you?" My smile spread wider, fierce and unapologetic. "Your days as a starter are numbered."

Craig's face flushed an ugly red, fists curling as he stepped forward like he might explode. "Shut your damn mouth."

I didn't flinch. "Or what? You gonna shove me into the boards, Craig? Take a cheap shot like you do on the ice?"

His chest heaved, his whole body vibrating with suppressed rage. But he didn't move. Because deep down, he knew I was right. And Trina's glossy veneer had cracked. She looked between us, doubt creasing her brow, her grip on Craig's arm a little less certain.

I let the moment stretch until it sang in the air, then I stepped back, my smirk as sharp as cut glass. "Now, if you'll excuse me, I have work to do."

With every ounce of pride left in me, I turned on my heel and walked away, my heart hammering like a war drum. I felt the eyes on my back as the weight of the moment settled like armor around my shoulders. But I didn't let it slow my stride. Vivi and Selene caught my eye as I passed, nodding with quiet pride. Vivi shot me a wink, and Selene's nod came with the quiet elegance of a queen giving silent approval, her heels clicking once she turned away.

As I reached the edge of the corridor, I threw one last glance over my shoulder. Craig stood frozen, fists clenched at his sides, his face still flushed and tight with barely swallowed fury. Trina wasn't looking at me anymore. Her gaze had shifted to him, narrowing with dawning suspicion, her arms falling away from him like she'd just realized she was standing on unstable ground.

A hush rippled through the small crowd of staff lingering nearby, the tension as thick as smoke. I let the image sear into my memory, a quiet triumph curling in my chest. Then I turned and walked away, my knees trembling but my spine straight.

I'd done it—I'd fought back. Let them deal with the fallout. I was done playing their games.

CHAPTER TWENTY-NINE

MAV

I wasn't the kind of guy who let things sit unresolved. Not on the ice, not in life, and sure as hell not when it came to Nyx.

She thought she had to handle everything alone, like asking for help was a weakness instead of survival. But not with me. Not anymore. She was carrying my kid. She was my wife—even if neither of us had planned it. And she didn't know it yet, but she wasn't going to fight this battle solo any longer. She was moving in—end of story.

"You mean to tell me," West drawled, arms crossed as he surveyed Nyx's tiny studio apartment, dim light filtering through grimy windows, "you married her, knocked her up, and now you're moving her in... without actually telling her?"

Sweat dampened my collar as I hefted a box marked Kitchen onto my shoulder. "You make it sound worse than it is."

"That's because it is worse." West didn't miss a beat.

His sharp gaze dragged over the bare-bones furnishings, the tired futon mattress, and the empty fridge door hanging open like even the leftovers had given up. We'd tried to turn on the lights—they hadn't worked. His jaw flexed.

Moving through the doorway with a grin like this was free entertainment, Hayes added, "Nah, man. This is premium reality-show material. Feels like we're two bad edits away from a Netflix scandal docuseries. Give it a week. Someone's getting a spinoff."

"Grab a box," I growled.

Their laughter followed me out the door as I hauled the load downstairs to the SUV. Without a cloud in the sky, the late-October sun heated the asphalt. Every step I took made my gut twist harder. Nyx had been living like this—half forgotten, fading into the cracks. No power. No food. No damn support. *Not anymore.*

We worked fast—quicker than it should've been, considering how little she had to her name—maybe an hour, tops. It took barely an hour to wipe out her life here, to carry the pieces of it to somewhere she could thrive.

"How's she gonna react," West asked, hauling the last box to the truck and slamming the tailgate shut, "when she walks in and sees her whole life unpacked in your place?"

I rolled my shoulders, tension tight across my back. "Bad. I expect yelling. Potentially my murder."

Hayes barked a laugh. "I like her already."

West cracked a grin, eyeing me over the truck's roof. "Hell, you keep pulling stunts like this, you'll have her breaking out the Taser in no time."

Anderson strolled up, flipping his sunglasses down over his eyes. "The man's a cautionary tale." He jerked a thumb at me. "First it's moving boxes, next it's Sunday farmers markets and couples' vision boards."

"Pinterest," Hayes chimed in. "Big Live, Laugh, Love energy."

"Real cute," I deadpanned, flipping them both off. But my mouth tugged into a grin.

The truth? I didn't give a damn. They could make fun of me all they wanted. The days of hookups and cheap shots during college after-parties were behind me. *Why would I want that just because I went into the NHL?* I didn't miss any of it. Not when I thought about Nyx—how she fought like hell to stand on her own, even when it nearly broke her.

My place felt different when we finished hauling her things into the condo. It felt lived-in, warmer, *ours*. Her books filled the shelves that had been empty this morning. Her throw blanket—a little frayed at the edges—draped over the back of my couch like it belonged there. Her jackets hung beside mine in the closet, her subtle citrus shampoo curling in the air.

West gave the space an approving once-over as he leaned against the island. "I'll give it to you, Davis. You actually made this look like a home."

"I know what I'm doing." I adjusted the final box near the kitchen island.

"Good," he shot back, slapping my shoulder. "Because if this goes sideways, we're blaming you."

Hayes winked as he headed for the door. "And I want front-row tickets to the drama."

"Get out," I muttered, but my grin lingered as they filed through the door, their laughter fading down the hall. I leaned across the threshold and yelled, "And… thank you!"

The door clicked shut behind them, and the condo fell quiet, a heavy, expectant kind of quiet. I dragged a hand over my face and paced a tight line between the couch and the kitchen, my pulse thick in my throat.

Every second crawled. Until I heard keys scrape in the lock. The door swung open, and Nyx stepped inside. She froze. Her gaze swept over the condo, the boxes broken down and stacked by the door, the newly filled bookshelves, the blanket on the couch, and the closet I hadn't yet shut with her jackets next to mine.

Her breath caught. "Mav," she said slowly, her voice dangerously calm. "What the hell is this?"

I straightened from where I'd been leaning against the counter. "Your stuff."

She set her bag down a little too hard, hands flying to her hips. "You—" Her eyes sparked. "You moved me in?"

I shrugged, unapologetic. "Yeah."

Her nostrils flared. "Without telling me?"

"You weren't gonna do it yourself."

"You can't just—" She broke off, pacing a sharp, furious line in front of the couch. "You *can't* just decide something like this for me, Mav!"

I pushed off the counter, closing the distance between us. "Yeah? Well, I just did."

Fire burned in her gaze. "You don't get to bulldoze your way into my life—"

"You're my wife."

The words hit the air like a thunderclap, thick and undeniable. She faltered. Just slightly. Her breath stuttered, her chest rising with a sharp inhalation.

"You're my wife," I said again, softer but no less confident. "And yeah, I don't exactly remember how the hell it happened, but it did. You're carrying my kid. And I know you didn't ask for this. I know you didn't want it to happen this way. But it did. And I'm not gonna sit back and watch you burn yourself out trying to survive when you don't have to struggle."

Her gaze darted to the boxes. Jaw tight, her throat working, she looked like she was swallowing words she couldn't speak. "I don't want to be a burden," she whispered.

"You're not."

Her eyes rose to mine, full of doubt and raw edges.

"You're not an obligation, Nyx." My voice roughened, dropping lower like I could make her believe it through sheer force of will. "You're my family. You and this baby. And I take care of family."

For a heartbeat, she didn't speak. I could see the war waging behind her eyes—the instinct to fight, to protect herself, colliding with the part of her that was tired of standing alone.

Finally, she blew out a breath and rubbed her temples, muttering, "You're impossible."

I let my grin curl slow and sure. "Yeah, but you're stuck with me."

A breath of a laugh slipped from her lips, tired, worn down, but real. It felt like winning the Stanley Cup.

Her gaze drifted to the nearest box I'd yet to unpack. Her fingers brushed the tape, a tremor ghosting through her hand before she steadied it. She pulled free one of her romance paperbacks, and her thumb grazed over the worn pages. Her voice came soft, almost to herself. "I can't believe you did all this."

I stepped closer, careful and deliberate. "Yeah," I said, my voice low and rough. "Because you belong here, Nyx. You always have."

Her eyes found mine—shining, unsure, but open. Vulnerability flickered beneath her usual armor, and she didn't pull away this time. Her breath slipped out on a shaky exhalation, shoulders softening.

I gently took the book from her hands and set it on the counter. Then I traced my knuckles along her jaw, brushing the corner of her mouth with my thumb. "Get used to it," I murmured. "Because I'm not going anywhere."

Her breath caught, eyes fluttering shut briefly before she opened them again. "Bossy," she whispered, but it held no heat.

"Told you." My grin deepened. "You're stuck with me."

Her mouth was still tilted in a half smile when I stepped in, close enough that her exhalation brushed my skin.

"We're really doing this, then?" she murmured.

I nodded, hands finding her waist. "It's already done. We're a team."

She rose onto her toes and kissed me—soft, hesitant for a

second before the tension snapped. I caught her with a low groan, my grip tightening as she pressed closer. Her mouth parted beneath mine, letting me in deeper, and I tasted every ounce of her resistance melting away.

Her hands slid up my chest, fisting the fabric of my shirt before tugging it over my head. I backed her into the counter, crowding her until her hips bumped the edge, then I lifted her—one smooth motion—and set her on top. Her legs locked around me like they'd always belonged there.

"Still mad at me?" I asked, peppering kisses along her jaw.

"Furious," she breathed, hips grinding into mine.

"Good." I kissed her again, rougher. "Use me to work it out."

She did.

Her nails scraped down my back as I kissed my way along her throat. I pulled her shirt off, exposing the soft swell of her breasts beneath a pale-pink lace bra. Dipping down, I kissed the skin just above the edge. I wound an arm around her narrow waist, lifted her, and in one swoop, pulled off her leggings and matching panties. She gasped when her skin met the cold quartz countertop. But then her eager fingers pushed at my waistband, hands trembling, and I helped her—freeing myself then finding her already wet and waiting.

"Don't be gentle," she whispered, eyes fierce.

I wasn't. I thrust in deep, swallowing her gasp with a kiss that turned ragged and messy. Her heels dug into my back as I moved, her body tightening around me like a vise. She met every stroke with urgency, her breath catching, her forehead pressed against mine.

"You're mine," I growled, hands gripping her hips. "Say it."

"Yes," she gasped. "Mav—God, yes."

"You're mine."

Her orgasm hit like a wave crashing, her whole body arching into me. I gritted my teeth as I chased my own release, slamming into her until I came, buried deep, every muscle locked with the force of it.

For a few long breaths, we didn't move. Her hands rested lightly on my shoulders, fingers tracing slow lines across my skin. My face pressed to her neck as I caught my breath, breathing her in as the world went quiet around us—just the sound of her heartbeat and mine, tangled in sync.

Eventually, I eased back, helping her down gently, brushing my hands across her hips like I couldn't stop touching her. She didn't pull away. She just looked at me, eyes soft, searching.

"I still hate that you did this without asking," she murmured, breathless.

"And I'd do it again," I said, kissing her hard and slow.

Her forehead dropped to chest, and her laugh came—warm and real, no walls left between us. We stood there, tangled in heat and quiet promises, the condo filled with the scent of her shampoo and the soft rustle of boxes stacked by the wall.

This was home. She was home. And no way in hell was I letting anyone take that away from us.

CHAPTER THIRTY

NYX

For the first time in a long while, I wasn't running. For longer than I could remember, my chest wasn't tight with the strain of it—of surviving, of dodging blows, of keeping my head barely above water while waiting for the next wave to crash down. In Mav's condo, morning sunlight spilling through the expansive windows and across the hardwood like a quiet tide, I could finally relax.

Outside, the California coastal breeze teased the curtains, carrying a faint tang of salt and ocean spray. Somewhere below, the sounds of the street filtered in—muted conversations, a distant bark of laughter, the low thrum of waves breaking against the California shoreline just a few blocks away.

I let my gaze drift over the space, taking in every quiet, telling detail that had begun to anchor me here. My books filled a shelf alongside Mav's old playbooks and sports biographies, the worn spines like old friends staking their claim. One of my soft throws—seafoam green and a little threadbare from too many moves—was draped over the back of the dark-gray couch. It was his space but mine too.

I crossed to the kitchen counter and ran my fingertips over

the cool stone surface. My chipped sunflower mug sat beside his protein shakes, a small but defiant burst of cheerfulness. Mav had brought it, a piece of my hastily boxed life. And yet, it felt like a quiet victory to see it among his things. Some part of me, deep and buried, had known this place wouldn't just be his for long.

Below the mug, I spotted a list in Mav's handwriting, messy but determined—crib options, pediatricians, babyproofing tasks. My throat caught, a tight knot forming as I traced a fingertip over the rough scrawl of his letters. I didn't doubt him, not anymore. He saw me—he saw *us*, even in the small details, but more than that, he wasn't waiting for me to carry this alone.

I opened the cabinet to find the prenatal vitamins he'd bought lined up in neat rows, like tiny sentries guarding my future. A small laugh broke from me, dry and surprised, as I picked up one of the bottles and turned it in my hand. Mav didn't do things halfway, not with hockey, not with life, and not with me.

The tension that had wrapped itself tight around my ribs since the day this all began eased, unfurling like a knot slowly coming undone. I set down the bottle and let my hand rest over my stomach, still flat but no less real. Life was there, quietly growing—small and invisible but undeniable.

I didn't push the thought away. I let it settle—the idea that this wasn't just mine to carry but a life taking shape, one that could have Mav's bright-blue eyes and his commanding confidence, or my blue-green eyes and my love of books. It would be growing into a future right there with us.

And the best part? I wasn't carrying my life, or this baby, in isolation anymore.

I wandered to the sliding door and tugged it wider to step out onto the small balcony. Breezy ocean air wrapped around me like a balm threaded with salt and sunlight. The breeze tangled my hair and kissed my skin. Below, the city moved at its usual rhythm, unaware of the turmoil that had raged inside me for months.

I inhaled deep, filling my lungs with the brine-sweet air, letting it anchor me to this moment and the life I'd never dared to hope for. For so long, I'd been braced for the worst. I had been conditioned to believe peace was just the brief silence before everything crumbled again. But here, in this sun-warmed space, with the echo of Mav's presence lingering in every corner, I felt acceptance and belonging, which was foreign, dangerous, and exhilarating. It was steady and quiet, like the tide rolling in against the shore. And I let it fill me. Not because I was naïve or believed the world outside these walls had forgotten about us.

My phone buzzed from where I'd left it on the counter, and I glanced at the screen flashing with another headline. I didn't even have to look. I already knew what it would say. The media nightmare wasn't over. Trina and Craig were out there, feeding the fire. They would continue circling, waiting for a crack to widen so they could tear me down and get Mav traded. We wouldn't let them. I refused to go down without a fight.

I stepped back inside and slid the door shut behind me. The latch clicked a final punctuation mark to the thought settling deep in my chest. The air inside smelled faintly like Mav's cologne—warm, clean, steady. Like a promise I hadn't dared to believe in before now.

For once, I wasn't bracing for impact. I was steadying for the fight. No longer the girl clinging to survival, a shadow at the edge of someone else's life. I was here. I was home. And when the next wave came, I wouldn't just stand my ground. I would meet it head-on.

The knock on the door startled me out of my thoughts. Three sharp raps then silence. Not the kind of knock you ignored—the kind that had intent.

I padded to the door, still in Mav's oversized hoodie, my hair shoved into a knot that could've passed for a small woodland creature. I cracked the door open just enough to peek through.

Selene arched one brow. "Really? You think we'd let you hide after *that* bombshell?"

Vivi leaned around her shoulder, holding up a bakery box with a shy smile. "We brought offerings—and questions, lots of questions."

I sighed, opening the door wider. "You couldn't have just texted?"

Selene breezed past me in a lavender wool coat that made her look like she was strutting onto a Paris runway, not invading my living room. "Oh, no, ma'am. This is not a textable offense. This is a sit-down, soul-baring, what-the-hell-happened-in-Vegas emergency conversation."

Vivi followed. Quietly, she set the pastry box on the kitchen counter like it was sacred. "We brought raspberry chocolate tarts. And cinnamon apple Danishes for you. We remember."

My chest tightened at that. I hadn't realized how much I missed this—the casual closeness, the comfort of people knowing your favorites.

"Tea," Selene demanded, flopping dramatically onto the couch and tossing a throw pillow into her lap. "Literal and metaphorical, spill both."

I hesitated in the kitchen, opening the box just to buy time. The scent of warm sugar and cinnamon hit me like a hug, instantly softening the panic curled under my ribs.

Vivi leaned on the island, watching me with those thoughtful blue eyes that always seemed to see past whatever I tried to hide. "We were hurt, Nyx—not because you owed us anything but because we care."

"I know," I said softly, tearing a Danish in half and handing it to her. "I wanted to tell you. I just... didn't know how."

"Try starting with, 'I got married in Vegas to the guy who got me pregnant and I'm now working for in secret,'" Selene said dryly. She bit into a pastry like it personally offended her.

I sank onto the couch across from her and tugged a throw blanket over my legs. "It wasn't planned."

Selene snorted. "Clearly."

"I mean, *really* not planned. I don't even remember the actual marriage event, elopement, whatever. There was alcohol. A lot of it. I woke up in his hotel suite with a hangover, a glittery fake veil, and a marriage certificate I found crumpled on the floor."

Vivi's mouth dropped open slightly. "*Wait.* You didn't know you would be working with him until *after?*"

"Not until weeks later. I left without telling him anything. I panicked."

Selene narrowed her eyes. "Did you... at least have fun? Before all the panic?"

Heat rushed to my cheeks. "I plead the Fifth."

"Oh, no you don't." Selene pointed a perfectly manicured finger at me. "You're married, Nyx. You *owe* us details. We've supported you through every Trina harassment and WAG-adjacent trauma. Give us something."

Vivi slid onto the edge of the couch and leaned in. "Was he— okay, was he *sweet drunk* or *chaos drunk?*"

My blush deepened. "A little of both. He danced with me in the middle of a crowded bar to a song I barely remember, sang karaoke, and laughed with me. He kissed me like he already knew me and whispered something about how I felt like his beginning."

Selene put a hand to her chest. "That's *rude.* You can't just drop a line like that and expect me not to cry."

Vivi fanned herself with a napkin. "Okay, so... he was charming?"

"Devastatingly," I admitted, barely above a whisper.

The beat of quiet was broken only by the crinkle of pastry paper and the soft hum of the heating vent.

Then Selene leaned forward. Her voice low but certain, she said, "You love him."

I didn't say anything. I didn't have to.

Vivi's voice was soft. "We're here, okay? You don't have to do this alone. Not the secrets, not the pregnancy, not the Trina-level drama. We've got you."

Emotion balled in my throat. I blinked hard and reached for my water, needing something to ground me. The glass was cool against my palm, the condensation slick between my fingers.

Selene's gaze softened, all her earlier sass giving way to that fierce, protective loyalty I'd missed so much. "And just so we're clear—if that man screws this up, I will fly to Vegas, find the chapel, and ask for a refund myself."

Vivi raised her pastry. "Seconded. And I'll key his car."

I let out a watery laugh. "You guys are insane."

Selene shrugged. "Insanely loyal."

I still had a dumpster fire to clean up, but at least I wouldn't be alone. Selene and Vivi were there—with opinions, sarcasm, and snacks. Which, honestly, might've been better than therapy. Nothing in my life was simple right now—but somehow, laughing with them made the mess feel a little less lonely. Maybe the only thing stronger than a secret marriage and a surprise baby was having friends who didn't flinch at either.

CHAPTER THIRTY-ONE

MAV

I was already on edge when I entered the locker room for today's game. And the second I glanced at my phone, I knew the bullshit was back in full swing. *Maverick Davis Caught in Scandal: Accidental Baby, Secret Marriage, a PR Nightmare?*

I exhaled, teeth clenching so hard my jaw ached. Same old media spin, different day. But I wasn't stupid; I knew where it came from—Trina and Ellis feeding the press whatever they could to make Nyx look like a mistake and to foster doubt about me with the league.

My thumb hovered over the screen. For a second, I debated calling Harper. But I didn't need to. A message already waited: *Press conference after the game. Manage the noise.*

She'd been telling me for a week we needed to get ahead of this. The public would keep writing their version of our story until we gave them the truth. *And after this headline?* I was done waiting.

Coach flagged me down before I could hit the ice, his ever-present coffee thermos tucked under one arm, a clipboard in the other. His jaw was tight, eyes sharp beneath the brim of his worn Titans hat. He took a slow sip from his battered thermos before speaking, eyes scanning me as if he could read my soul. "You good?" he asked, his voice low. "Because if you're not, I need to know before this becomes another Jennings situation."

"I'm good," I said. "Just tired of people twisting the story."

He gave a slow nod. "You're delivering where it counts, and I've backed you at every step. But we've got sponsors, media, and management circling like sharks lately. I can't afford to put out another fire."

"I've got it handled."

His eyes held mine a second longer, then he nodded once, firmly. "Good. Then do what you're paid to do"—his gaze flicked to the ice and the packed stands—"then manage it."

***

Nyx

The arena never truly slept. Even now, after the final horn had faded and the crowd had poured into the cool California night, the building hummed with life beneath my feet. Zambonis groaned over the ice, leaving mirrored swaths behind them. Somewhere down the corridor, equipment managers packed away sweat-soaked gear. The clatter of sticks and skate guards echoed against the lingering echoes of post-game adrenaline.

I stood at the side entrance of the press room, laptop tucked under my arm, phone tight in my hand, not by accident. Their chatter was loud, every seat filled by an eager reporter.

The win had been tight, hard-earned, and ugly, like grinding out a victory with clenched teeth and a pulse in the throat. Relief wasn't the word for it—it felt more like a brief pause in the chaos, a shallow breath before the next storm rolled in.

My phone buzzed against my palm. *Rookie Star Davis: Is Domestic Life Costing Him His Rookie Focus?*

The headline twisted in my stomach like a blade. Not subtle. Not even close. The narrative had shifted from intrigue to accusation. And I didn't need a leak report to know where it originated—Craig and Trina. They didn't care if they set fire to the whole damn world so long as they stayed warm from the blaze.

Across the room, Kieran St. James entered like he owned the space, his damp hair curled at the ends from the shower, his jersey swapped for team-issued gear, sleeves pushed to his elbows. His gaze scanned the press until it landed on me, directly and deliberately.

A slow, crooked smile curved his mouth as he strode over. "You here to spy on us, Lawson?"

I lifted a brow, holding up my phone between two fingers. "Here to stay ahead of the headlines," I said evenly. "I'd rather know what they're saying before it hits Mav's mentions."

His smile deepened, approving. "Smart," he murmured, sounding low and rough, as his gaze flicked toward the reporters gathering like vultures. "They're circling tonight."

A pulse ticked in my throat, tight beneath my skin. "Let them."

The assistant coach stepped to the front of the room, clearing his throat to call for attention. Chairs scraped against the floor as reporters settled in like predators scenting blood.

Kieran's eyes lingered on me for half a second longer, a quiet steel in his look. Like he wanted me to know he saw me— *really* saw me—and not as a bystander. He gave a short nod then turned toward the table beneath the sharp glow of media lights. He looked every inch the team's anchor—solid, unshaken, unbreakable.

I stayed where I was, back against the wall, phone warm in my grip, my pulse thudding in my ears as the first question fired.

"Kieran St. James," a reporter began, polite enough on the

surface but sharp beneath. "Congrats on the win. Tight game out there. Would you say the team's rhythm has been off lately?"

Kieran's jaw flexed. "Hockey's about adjusting. No team's perfect every night, but we play to win—and that's what we did." His answer was smooth, controlled.

But they weren't done.

Another reporter leaned in, eyes glinting. "There's talk Davis's personal life is creating distractions for the team. Marriage, fatherhood, rookie-year pressure—has that affected focus on the ice?"

The words hit me like a slap, hot prickles skimming my skin. I kept my expression flat, my spine straight.

The veins on Kieran's tattooed forearm flexed as he gripped the mic, but his voice stayed firm. "Davis plays with more focus than half the guys in this league," he shot back. "You want distractions? Try injuries and power-play turnovers. His family? Not one of them."

There it was—the defense, clean and hard-edged.

Still, the reporter pressed. "But the adjustment—"

Kieran cut him off without missing a beat. "Funny thing," he said almost conversationally, "when one of our other guys had his first kid, no one asked that question. Strange, huh?"

An uncomfortable ripple went through the room. Then another reporter pounced, eyes flicking to me at the side entrance to the room. "So you'd say Nyx Lawson hasn't changed the dynamic for Davis?"

Kieran's gaze rose to mine, direct and as steady as a heart-beat. "She's part of this team," he answered, his voice tight with conviction. "She keeps things running so Davis can focus where it counts. She's not the problem—she's the backbone."

The words struck harder than I expected, massaging old scars I didn't realize were still tender. The weight of his words slammed into me like armor settling over my chest. I held his gaze, a flicker of warmth blooming under my skin.

The reporter opened his mouth to follow up—but the side door behind me creaked open. Every head turned, including mine. Mav was still in half his gear, damp from the game, jaw tight. His eyes scanned the room, finding mine in an instant. And there, the fire in his gaze softened for just a beat. He looked at me like I was the only thing tethering him to the earth.

Kieran left the podium, passing me on his way out. He didn't stop, but his words brushed my ear like a promise. "You're more than part of this, Lawson."

Not reassurance. Truth. I took it, let it settle in my bones where fear had once lived.

Kieran slapped Mav on the shoulder. "Go get 'em."

Then, a breath later, cutting through the room like he didn't see anyone else, Mav was in front of me. His eyes locked on mine, serious and fierce. "You good?" His voice was low, rough, threaded with something possessive and protective.

I didn't hesitate. I didn't need to. "Yeah." I held his gaze without wavering. "I'm better than good."

The corner of his mouth twitched, just a hint of a smile, pride simmering beneath it. He brushed his knuckles over mine in a subtle, grounding touch that sent a warm current racing through me. "Good," Mav murmured, his eyes never leaving mine. "Because we're just getting started."

My breath caught—not from fear, from fire. *Let them circle. Let them try because they'd underestimated me for the last time.*

Mav

The press conference was set up in one of the media rooms at the arena—bright lights, too many cameras. I told Nyx she didn't need to come, but she'd shown anyway, arms crossed, her expression unreadable. She looked like she was bracing for war. I wasn't going to let them touch her.

I stepped up to the podium. In an even voice, I said, "I'll make this quick. There's been a lot of speculation about my personal life lately. About my wife, Nyx, our relationship, and the baby."

A ripple of anticipation moved through the reporters. I gripped the podium's edge, the cool metal grounding me as the lights flared hotter than they should've.

"The truth is, this isn't a scandal. It's my life. Nyx isn't an opportunist, and this isn't a PR stunt. She's my wife. We got married in Vegas a little over a month ago. It wasn't planned, but that doesn't make it a mistake."

Nyx stiffened slightly at that, her eyes wide. But I didn't stop.

"And yeah, we're having a baby. It's not something we expected, but we're both very happy about it. So if you're looking for a controversy, you won't find one here."

Questions came quickly. "So, you're confirming the marriage? You and Nyx are officially together?"

"Again, yes."

"Do you think this will affect your focus on the ice?"

I pinned the guy with a look like he was an opponent in the way of scoring a goal. This guy seemed to be the most vocal, which meant he was probably Ellis's go-to source.

He looked down at his notes, flustered.

Good. "I'm here to play hockey. Nothing changes that. But I'm also not about to let the media drag my wife or kid into a circus just because it makes good headlines."

The assistant coach saw his chance and ended the session cleanly. "That's all for tonight."

Chairs scraped, notebooks shut, and the buzz of conversation filled the space like static.

I walked off before they could ask more questions. Harper stepped in, heels clicking against the floor as she took a stance at the podium to do the wrap-up like a general collecting the trophies from a war she'd already won. No spin, no fluff.

Nyx met me offstage, arms still crossed. "You didn't have to do that," she said, her voice quiet.

I held her gaze. "Yeah, I did." Deep down, I knew she'd needed someone to choose her out loud, and I always would.

Her throat worked. "Mav—"

"I meant what I said. You're my wife. And I won't let anyone make you feel like you don't belong here."

Her gaze softened, and she nodded slowly. "Thank you."

It wasn't much. But it was a start. The next step was dealing with the other problem—her so-called family. I pressed a too-brief kiss to her soft lips. "I've got to check in with Coach and watch some film before I can meet you at home. Are you leaving now?"

"Yeah, I think so. I'm pretty tired, and we're going to visit your parents tomorrow."

I squeezed her hand before letting her go, despite how much I wanted to pull her into my arms and let the rest of the world burn. She wasn't just a passing addiction. She was my everything, despite the whirlwind of how things had happened for us. I waited in the hall, reluctant to head to Coach's office, just watching as she walked away, wishing I could go with her.

CHAPTER THIRTY-TWO

MAV

The cold in Illinois was a bit harsher than I remembered. It had a way of cutting through layers no matter how tightly you wrapped yourself, settling into breath and bone. As I steered the rental off the main road and into my parents' neighborhood, the sky hung heavy with steel-gray clouds, and the bungalows we passed hunched like old men against the winter chill. A dusting of snow covered the edges of cracked sidewalks, and the trees with straggling brown leaves stood like skeletal sentinels.

Beside me, Nyx cupped her hands around her to-go tea, her gloves rested on her lap, and her fingers paled from the cold. She hadn't said much since we left the airport, but her quiet wasn't distant. It was weighted, careful, like she was holding her breath right along with me.

"This is it," I murmured, turning the car onto my parents' street, tires crunching over patches of frost. I kept my eyes forward, my voice a notch lower. "Right there—that's Coach Becket's place."

I flicked my chin toward the brown house with the faded Fall Lake University *Go Falcons!* banner drooping in the window. The brick two-story had always seemed like a beacon of light in my life. "Skye lived there," I added, watching Nyx's eyes follow my line of sight. "After her parents passed when she was young, she moved in with her aunt and uncle. That house was like a second home for me."

Nyx's gaze lingered on it, a quiet furrow forming between her brows. "She's in Kansas now, right? Since Liam got drafted."

"Yeah." My throat tightened, memories stacking fast and full behind my ribs. "Kansas City. They just moved into a place out there with Lily, and…" I almost smiled. "They're expecting another."

Her expression softened, as if she could see the parallel without me saying what it meant for people to build a future from ashes.

We didn't linger. I eased the car into my parents' driveway, the house at the end of the block looking smaller than it used to. The oak tree out front had lost its leaves, its brittle branches clawing at the overcast sky.

My pulse thudded against my collarbone as I killed the engine. "You okay?" The words came rough, tighter than I intended.

She exhaled softly, steam curling from her breath. "Are you?"

I answered without thinking. "Ask me after."

Before she could reach for the handle, I was out of the car, rounding to her side, and popping open the door. Her gaze caught on mine, a flicker of surprise crossing her face, but she didn't pull away when I covered her ice-cold fingers with my own and helped her to her feet. She squeezed once, small but certain. I threaded our fingers together, taking advantage of any excuse to touch her.

The steps up to the porch groaned under our weight. Wind chimes rattled above, and the bite of winter clung to the air. I knocked once, my chest as tight as a drum. The door opened almost instantly.

"Maverick," my mom breathed, pulling me into a hug before I could blink.

She felt thinner in my arms, the edges of her frame fragile beneath her sweater. But her grip was still strong and full of familiar, unrelenting love.

When she pulled back, her eyes landed on Nyx, and her expression softened. "You must be Nyx. It's so nice to put a face to the voice finally. We've talked enough on the phone that I feel like I know you already."

My brows rose. I knew they'd spoken a few times when Nyx was booking flights for me during the rare windows I could get home throughout the season, but seeing how my mom smiled at her, I realized they must've bridged the gap and become closer than polite strangers.

Nyx stood steady beside me, voice clear. "Hi, Amanda."

My mom's smile warmed, and she waved us both inside. "Come in before you freeze."

We shrugged out of our coats and shoes, the warmth of the house slowly chasing off the last of the cold. The dining table was already set—Mom's handiwork, no doubt. A pot roast with potatoes and vegetables waited, filling the space with the kind of comfort only a childhood home could provide.

The house smelled like lemon cleaner and winter dust from when the heat turned on. The photos on the wall were the same. The faded floral couch still sat in the living room, but a shadow hung over everything—a quiet pall cast by the sight of my dad in his recliner.

His skin was pale, his frame smaller than I remembered, and a blanket had been pulled tight over his lap. But his bright-blue eyes, their color identical to mine, still burned with the same stubborn fire I'd known my whole life.

"About damn time," he rasped, his voice rough but unmistakably his. "I was starting to think you forgot where you came from."

"Wouldn't dare," I said, crossing the room to clasp his hand. His grip was weaker than it had once been, but it was solid beneath the frailty.

His gaze shifted to Nyx, curiosity flickering beneath his fatigue. "And this beautiful young lady?"

She stepped forward. "I'm Nyx."

After introductions, Dad moved to the table, and conversation resumed cautiously. Hockey came up first. My latest game. A comment about a scuffle on the ice that my dad had clearly rewound and watched three times.

"You've got to keep your gloves on, son," he muttered, even as pride tugged at the corner of his mouth.

I grinned. "You taught me better than to bare-knuckle brawl. But sometimes guys need reminding. The games have been going well, though."

Nyx smiled beside me, her fork toying with the roasted carrots on her plate. "He's being modest. He got two assists and a short-handed goal in that game."

Dad raised a brow, eyes flicking to me. "That so? We've got another hockey fan in our midst."

Mom's soft laugh filled the space. "She's got the stats memorized already. Looks like you've got yourself a *true* fan."

We talked about Skye and Liam, how quickly their little girl was growing. Dad brought up Coach Becket and my old coach before he asked about Fall Lake's season this year.

Then he shifted slightly in his seat and murmured, "I'm tired a little more often. But the treatments are holding—for now." He said it plainly, with the kind of quiet resolve he'd always carried.

I swallowed around the tightness in my throat. "You look good, Dad."

"I feel... all right." He pointed his fork at me. "And don't think we didn't hear the rumblings."

My pulse ticked up. "What rumblings?"

Mom arched a brow. "People talk, Mav. But we don't take stock in gossip. We figured if something important happened, we'd hear it from you."

Her voice held no accusation, just quiet certainty. It made my chest ache.

They watched my games, but they made a point of staying away from any of the gossip. And with the treatments and the worry they were constantly under, I hadn't doubted they were unaware of what'd been circling through the sports-world gossip.

I slid closer to Nyx and pressed my hand on the small of her back. "Yeah," I confirmed, the truth steady in my chest. "Nyx is my wife. I—we—wanted to wait and tell you in person."

The words landed heavily in the room like thunder rolling in from the horizon. My mom froze, lips parting.

My dad's brows shot up, his eyes widening like he wasn't sure he heard right. "So it's true." A beat of silence followed, then my dad's rough laugh broke it. "Well, hell," he said, shaking his head, a faint glimmer of pride creeping through his grin. "You always were full throttle."

My mom let out a breath that was equal parts laugh, disbelief, and something I didn't want to name yet. We got up from the table, and Mom ushered us deeper into the living room, gesturing for us to sit.

Once we eased onto the couch, we dove into our story, keeping it light and telling them pieces of what had happened—Vegas, the surprise, the way everything had unfolded like a playbook with too many audibles. Nyx's laugh came easy once we got going, and my parents soaked it in, clinging to it like sunlight breaking through clouds.

Finally, when the moment felt right, I laced my fingers through Nyx's, grounding both of us. "There's more," I said, my voice quieter but sure.

My dad's brow arched. My mom's gaze sharpened.

"You're gonna be grandparents." The words left my chest, not as a bombshell but as a promise.

For a breath, the room stilled.

Then my dad's chest hitched, rising slow on an inhalation that felt like it scraped every inch of his ribs. "Grandfather," he intoned, tasting the word like it was sacred. His eyes glistened, and something inside me cracked wide open.

My mom's hands flew to her mouth as tears filled her eyes. She turned to Nyx. In a voice thick with emotion, she said, "Welcome to the family, sweetheart."

Nyx's breath caught, her eyes bright, but she didn't falter. She met my mom's gaze head-on, her fingers tightening around my mother's. "Thank you," she whispered, her voice steady and sure.

Pride swelled sharply in my chest, fierce and protective.

"You've always had a way of running headfirst into the unknown," my dad rasped, pride roughening his voice. "And you built yourself a damn good life."

I couldn't speak past the knot in my throat. I just nodded, my arm sliding around Nyx's waist, anchoring her to me and this moment.

The sky was inky when we pulled away from my parents' house, the chill outside turning brutal enough that the windshield fogged at the edges, ghosting our reflections across the glass.

For the first few minutes, neither of us spoke.

Nyx sat with her knees drawn up a little, the seat warmer turned to high beneath her, her arms folded over her middle like she was still holding onto the gravity of my mom's words, "Welcome to the family, sweetheart." I knew how much that meant to her, having lost her dad over a year ago and living through the betrayal of the only family she had left.

Her gaze tracked the darkened houses as we passed them,

the muted glow of porch lights, and the empty streets dusted with frost. But she wasn't looking at any of them.

"You're quiet," I said, my voice low in the hush of the car.

She blinked like she'd been pulled from someplace deep. "So are you."

Fair enough. My hands flexed on the steering wheel. I didn't want to let the weight of tonight settle like ice between us. I didn't want her to carry even an ounce of doubt when we'd taken a more significant step than we had probably realized until now.

"Thank you," she said suddenly, her voice soft but steady.

I flicked my gaze to her. "For what?"

"For not rushing through it," she answered, her eyes still on the passing houses. "For letting it be real. For letting them see me."

Her words hit me square in the chest. I reached over and laced my fingers through hers where they sat in her lap, our joined hands warm in the space between. "They would've seen you no matter what," I told her, my voice gruff. "But I'm glad you experienced it too."

Her breath caught just a little before she exhaled slowly. "I did."

She turned her head then, looking at me fully, and in the soft glow of the dashboard lights, her eyes were open in a way they hadn't been before—not guarded, not wary. "I want this, Mav," she said so quietly it felt like a vow.

My pulse kicked, not from surprise—but from something deeper. Like her words lit a match in my chest. "So do I," I told her, my thumb stroking over her knuckles, slow and sure. "Every damn part of it."

The tension in her shoulders eased, her breath steadying. She didn't look away. And in that moment, in the quiet of the car, as we headed to the airport, in the frozen Midwest dark, it felt like we'd fully turned a corner.

CHAPTER THIRTY-THREE

NYX

It'd only been a few minutes since we'd arrived at Mav's condo after our flight, and both of us were wiped. We'd collapsed onto the couch, and he'd idly picked up the remote but hadn't turned on the TV.

I leaned into him then cupped the side of his jaw, wanting to ease the exhaustion there, and his lips curved in a soft smile. Since we'd met, there had been a magnetic pull between us, impossible to resist. And now that everything was out in the open—the marriage, the baby—there was no longer a reason to fight it. No more hiding in shadows. *So why should I?*

My thumb brushed across his brow, smoothing the line of tension etched there. The pads of my fingers followed the curve of his cheekbone and his rough stubble. He was warm beneath my hand. Solid. Real in a way that made my chest ache.

I needed this—more than I could ever admit aloud. The danger wasn't in the touch itself. It was in what came next, in what had been building beneath my ribs since our first kiss. His eyes searched mine, and I knew he saw me. Not the guarded version I let the world see. He saw every crack, every jagged piece I tried to hold together.

"I love you, you know." He said it softly, like he didn't want to scare me off.

The words landed like a punch to the chest—not sharp, not violent, but sudden and devastatingly deep, like the air had been ripped from my lungs, leaving me weightless and unmoored. I froze, my fingers still against his jaw, but everything inside me fractured. My pulse thundered in my ears.

I wanted to say it back. God, I wanted to tell him I felt it, too —buried deep beneath my fear, tangled up in every heartbeat between us. But the words stuck in my throat, heavy with every time love had turned to pain. Since my dad had passed, love had been a weapon in my life, used to control. Used to break. And now, staring into Mav's eyes, it felt like it could be something incredible. But still—I couldn't force the words past my lips.

Mav didn't flinch. He didn't push. He simply watched me, his gaze steady and sure, as if he already knew my answer, even if I couldn't give it a voice. That made it worse. Because it meant he understood. It meant he saw the fight inside me and loved me anyway.

His exhalation was quiet, as if he hadn't expected anything in return, as if giving me his truth was enough. No strings. No demands. And that cracked something open in me all over again.

The condo fell into a hush, night settling deeper around us, long shadows painting the walls as time held still. I drew in a slow breath, my chest tight, and turned away before I shattered completely. After crossing to the window, I pressed my palm to the cool glass. Outside, the horizon had long since swallowed the sun, darkness bleeding in to take its place like ink across the water.

Behind me, I sensed him watching, his quiet patience and steady presence filling the space between us.

I wanted to say it back. God, I *would* say it back. I wasn't there yet—but I was closer than ever because I'd finally found someone worth being brave for.

I let my gaze trace the fading line of the sun until it disappeared beyond the horizon, my heart settling into a quiet promise. Not yet. But soon.

CHAPTER THIRTY-FOUR

NYX

Mav's large hand enveloped mine as he helped me from his SUV. We'd arrived at the venue where the Literacy Gala was being held—a charity event attended by the who's who of the hockey world and the surrounding elite. I smoothed a shaky hand down the silky fabric of my midnight-blue gown, loving how it shimmered subtly under the streetlights. The fitted bodice hugged every curve while the flowing skirt danced with each step. Mav had surprised me with it earlier, but he refused to take credit. Apparently, he'd enlisted help—from none other than Jenson Rhodes's and Kieran St. James's wives.

The press of his muscular body, tall and protective, warmed me as we ascended the red carpet that graced the marble steps of the hotel. Camera flashes lit the entrance, shouting our arrival to the world, whether we wanted it or not.

As we stepped through the grand doors into the lobby, I couldn't help sneaking glances at him out of the corner of my eye. He was devastating in a custom black suit, the crisp lines accentuating his broad chest and tapered waist. His jaw was freshly shaven, his hair styled just enough to look effortlessly perfect. Heads turned as we passed, but he didn't seem to notice.

I did. And a surge of fierce possession swept through me. My fingers squeezed his biceps.

"You okay?" Mav dipped his head, catching my eyes.

"Yeah," I smiled tightly. "Just nervous. This is a huge event, and… everyone will be here."

Something dark flashed in his electric-blue eyes. He understood without me having to say it—Trina, Craig… maybe even Cynthia.

The ballroom sparkled like a dream. Crystal chandeliers floated overhead like glittering stars. Round tables draped in white-and-silver linens fanned out around the dance floor, each one set with gold-rimmed glassware and carefully placed name cards. Servers in black uniforms carried trays of champagne. Even the air smelled expensive—soft florals and lavish perfume mixed with aged wood and waxed floors.

A sudden gasp beside me broke the tension.

"You made it!" Vivi squealed, throwing her arms around me. Her dark curls tickled my cheek as she hugged me tightly.

Jenson greeted Mav on the other side with a warm clap on the back while Selene pulled me into another embrace, her smile lit with approval.

"Girl, I *knew* that dress was going to look amazing on you." Selene stepped back to admire it. "Mav texted us a photo of the options. I told him he better go with this one."

Vivi linked arms with me. "She's been waiting all night to see it on you."

We laughed, and for a moment, I felt… safe. Happy. Like maybe tonight could just be about us. Then Selene stiffened slightly, her gaze flicking past my shoulder.

Vivi followed her line of sight. "Don't look now…" she whispered.

I turned anyway. Trina had arrived, hand in hand with Craig. Her blond hair was twisted into an elaborate updo, and her red gown sparkled like freshly spilled blood. My stepmother, Cynthia, wasn't far behind, escorted by a man I didn't recognize—a new boyfriend, I guessed. She wore her usual air of elegance, thin-lipped and disapproving as if the whole event was beneath her. My stomach turned.

Mav leaned in close. "Ignore them. You've got me, remember?"

The gala moved forward quickly. Our table buzzed with laughter and inside jokes. Selene teased Kieran for silently bidding fifteen grand on a signed guitar he didn't know how to play. Vivi kept eyeing the dessert table like it owed her money, whispering that if dinner didn't come soon, that was where we would start. Harper swung by for a quick hello and gave Mav a nod of approval before disappearing again.

When the auction portion started, I was stunned by how much money was raised in under an hour. Trips, autographed jerseys, one-of-a-kind experiences—each item selling for more than I would make in a year. Even Mav threw his name in once, outbidding someone on an evening dinner cruise.

Then came the dancing.

Mav's hand found mine, and he led me onto the floor. The music was smooth and elegant—something jazzy with a rhythm I could melt into. I relaxed into his arms, the world blurring around us as we swayed together.

"This is nice," I said softly, cheek brushing his shoulder.

"Yeah," he murmured. "Almost makes me forget where we are."

But reality slammed back when we stepped off the dance floor and Craig shoulder checked Mav as we passed.

"Watch it," Craig muttered, not looking back.

Trina let out a shrill laugh, clutching Craig's arm like they were onstage.

Mav stilled.

I touched his arm. "Let it go."

Trina turned then, all venom masked as elegance. "Isn't this cozy? The fairy tale continues."

I turned to face her. "Don't."

She smirked. "You think putting on a gown makes you one of us?"

Cynthia broke from the couple she was conversing with and stepped forward, lips pursed. "We don't need to make a scene."

"We're *already* in one," Mav said tightly.

Trina's lips curved into a smirk. "Oh, come on. Don't be like that. I just wanted to say congratulations. After all, not many women can pull off a stunt like Nyx did and come out on top."

Mav stepped in before I could respond. "You need to walk away, Trina."

Trina's eyes flicked to Mav, and I saw a crack in her confidence. She hadn't expected him to intervene.

"This is between me and my sister," she said, her voice tighter.

"She's my wife," Mav said flatly. "So whatever you think you need to say, you can say to me."

Trina's eyes flashed with annoyance, but she recovered quickly. "You really think this is forever, Mav? That she won't run the second it benefits her?"

He didn't even blink. "I think you're projecting."

I made a noise in my throat, like I was half choking on a laugh. Trina's smirk wavered.

"You've spent your whole life making her feel like she's less than you," Mav continued, his tone calm but unyielding. "But guess what? She doesn't need you. And she sure as hell doesn't need Ellis, no matter how much he wishes she wanted him." He drove the nail home. "A person would have to be blind not to see the way he objectifies her."

"Please." Trina scoffed, but I could see the cracks widening. "Stop with your lies."

My turn. I took a step forward. "I used to think I needed your love and acceptance," I said, my voice quieter but no less strong. "I used to think I needed this family." I inhaled deeply. "But I don't."

Trina's composure slipped further. Her smile turned brittle. "You think you've won something? You were never supposed to last with the Titans. That's the whole reason I let you work for him. You were supposed to screw it up, make a scene, prove to everyone you couldn't do it."

My eyes flared, but I wasn't surprised. Just… tired. "And yet, here I am. Still standing. Still not who you expected."

Trina's lips parted like she had more to say, but nothing came out.

"So this is me telling you—I'm done," I said firmly. "Keep your toxicity. Keep your judgments. I'm moving on."

Trina's expression twisted, but she didn't argue. Because she knew she'd lost.

Craig crossed his arms. He took up for Trina when she was silent. "Heard the press is eating it up. You really are milking this for all it's worth, Nyx."

I bristled. "Excuse me?"

Trina stepped in, her confidence back, reinforced by Craig's support. "Oh, come on, Nyx. You always were a good actress. Playing the victim. Crying to Daddy. Now you're trying to upgrade to a hockey wife and hanging with them too." Her gaze flicked off to the side where Vivi and Selene were making their way toward us. "It's pathetic that you think any of your attempts to manipulate people could be a permanent solution. He'll get tired of you in no time."

My voice dropped. "Excuse me? That's pretty ironic, considering you're engaged to a hockey player whose attention so easily wanders." I bit my tongue, inwardly groaning at the slip.

Trina edged closer, her temper flaring as two red spots appeared on her cheeks. "What's that supposed to mean?"

"Please, like you don't know who you're marrying." I hissed. "Like you don't know what he did to me."

"You're jealous and a liar. Everyone knows it," Craig cut in, his tone edged with too much panic to discredit me before the truth could come out, though he was clearly trying.

My heartbeat thundered in my ears. For a split second, I was nineteen again, scared, trapped, and humiliated. Then I saw Mav's hand clench at his side, and Vivi's face twisted in shock. I remembered the girl who survived, and I found my voice.

"You think I don't remember?" I stepped forward, into Craig's space. "You reeked of whiskey as you locked the door. You said I needed someone to show me what I was worth. And when I shoved you off, you said I'd made a huge mistake but I would come around." A kiss taken was so very different than one given—and he'd been all about force.

Trina's face drained of color as silence fell.

"*What?*" Vivi gasped from beside me.

Craig scoffed. "That's not—"

Mav's jaw ticked, and I saw it—that barely leashed rage just beneath the surface. Not the hotheaded kind. No, this was the controlled, dangerous fury of a man who knew precisely what had been taken from me. And he wouldn't let it slide.

"I told her," I said to Craig then turned to Trina. "But you didn't care. You blamed *me*. You said I was trying to ruin your relationship. Just like you ruined every good thing I ever had."

"Nyx," Cynthia cut in sharply, her voice taut with warning. "You're hysterical. You're drunk—"

The word stung like a slap. The way my stepmother said it— dismissive and smug—like she could rewrite the past with a single lie and still shame me into silence.

"I'm pregnant," I snapped. "I haven't had a drink tonight, and I wasn't drunk then either."

Mav's voice thundered beside me. "If you knew anything about Nyx, you would know she wouldn't lie about something like that. But you all would. Cynthia, you cut her off after her father died. Hijacked his estate and threw her out of her own home."

Gasps rippled around us. Chairs scraped as guests twisted to face us.

One man who had spent an ungodly amount of money tonight murmured, "Despicable."

People started to gather, drawn by the confrontation. Whispers turned into audible outrage. They were finally seeing it. Not the woman Cynthia painted herself and her daughter to be but the one who had turned my grief into a weapon and used it against me.

Cynthia's face became leeched of all color, and her new boyfriend took a step back, putting distance between them. Her eyes narrowed, hatred darkening them further. Trina's lower lip trembled as her gaze darted around the growing crowd of onlookers.

A woman in a green sequined dress leaned toward her husband. "Cynthia Lawson is her stepmother? The one who's always front row of the fundraisers?"

Another guest, someone I vaguely recognized from the country club I used to go to when Dad was alive, pulled out her phone. "This is going viral," she said, not even bothering to lower her voice.

Cynthia stood there, spine stiff, eyes darting like a cornered animal's. Her mask was slipping, and people were watching as it fell.

"Bet her father's friends don't know what you've been up to, do they?" Mav continued. "That while you wore his last name and smiled from your ivory tower, you treated his daughter like an inconvenience. Like garbage. She's not your victim. She never was. But you should know we all see the truth now—every lie you fed her, every dollar you stole, every time you looked the other way. And it's over."

"She was in college then, not even employed, basically a kid," Selene said as she flanked my other side, her voice like steel.

"How could you?" another woman snapped at Cynthia, clutching her husband's arm.

The murmurs grew louder. A couple who had been sitting at Cynthia and Trina's table stood and moved away. Even the wait-staff paused, eyes wide and alert as the scandal unraveled in real time.

"You covered for Craig, for your mom," I said, voice shaking but clear as my gaze landed on Trina. "You let them treat me like a mistake. You *chose* to believe Craig when I stood up for myself, then you and your mom made me pay for it. He hasn't changed, Trina." She needed to hear the truth. No matter how much I despised her, not telling her about seeing Craig with Lara didn't sit right with me. "You might want to ask Lara. She and Craig seemed awfully close when I saw them together last."

Trina gasped, her head reeling back like she'd been slapped before she whirled on Craig.

Cynthia looked like she might faint, but no one stepped in to help her or Trina. Not this time.

Mav slid his arm around my waist. "We're done here."

As we turned, the crowd parted around us. Trina stepped away from Craig as her mask shattered. Cynthia wavered on her heels, struggling to breathe beneath the weight of her unraveling lies as the crowd distanced themselves from the trio. No one defended them or tried to smooth things over. They were radioactive.

As I walked away from that nightmare with Mav by my side, I didn't look back. I felt weightless. The burden they'd hung around my neck for years—guilt, fear, shame—slipped off my shoulders like a cloak I never chose to wear. Maybe tonight hadn't been about glitz or gowns but about finally burning down the house they'd locked me in. And building something real with the man who chose, believed in, and saw me.

CHAPTER THIRTY-FIVE

NYX

Game night meant packed stands, bright lights, and the bite of tension in the air. The kind that made every pass and play feel bigger than just a game. The energy inside the arena was electric—that humming, thunderous current that seeped into the bones.

I found my seat in the family section and slid in beside Vivi and Selene. My fingers curled around the bottled water I'd pulled from my bag. Vivi had popcorn already balanced on her lap, and Selene was snapping a picture of the ice.

"Mav's starting," I murmured, mostly to myself, but Vivi overheard and grinned.

"Damn right he is," she said. "They'd be idiots not to put him on the first line after that last game."

"Have you seen the stat sheet?" Selene added. "He's already outpacing the other rookies by a mile."

I tried to smile and steady my breathing, but it was hard. I was anxious despite how Mav always owned the ice.

The face-off snapped into motion, and the game began with bone-rattling energy. Mav tore across the ice, fast and fluid, weaving through defenders like they were standing still. The puck rode his stick like an extension of his hand. He passed clean and chased harder. It was the kind of play that turned heads.

"Did you see that pass?" Selene breathed.

"He's on fire," Vivi said halfway through her popcorn.

We were caught up in it—the rhythm of the game, the power of it—until Craig happened.

It started on the bench. I could see his jaw tighten, his posture coiled with something more than just adrenaline. The cameras weren't on him, but my eyes were. I knew that look.

A shift change put Mav on the ice at the same time as Craig. The tension was instant.

They passed each other at the boards without a word. Nothing needed to be said.

Then Craig slammed his stick hard as Mav cut in for a breakaway. It was subtle, just enough to slip past the officials but enough for Mav to feel the slight. Players on the same team didn't go after each other—there were codes and unspoken rules of brotherhood on the ice, not to mention professional-ism. I mean, they were on the same damn team with goals aligned, allies despite personality differences. But Craig had already broken too many of those codes. This wasn't about the game anymore. It was personal, and it was boiling over.

The second period was just as ruthless. Every time Mav was on the ice, Craig found an excuse to get too close to take any passes sent by Mav—a slash here, a bump there. Just enough to stir the pot.

It was off a line change when things boiled over. They collided near the boards, too close, too hard. It looked like a scrap for the puck—until Craig shoved Mav with two hands to the chest after the play.

Gloves dropped.

"Shit," I hissed, standing halfway as the crowd exploded.

What did this say about the team? "Avoid scandal"? That'd been the motto—this violated all the warnings. It made everyone look bad, and the coaches wouldn't let it slide.

"Ellis started it," Selene said.

"Davis's going to finish it," Vivi replied.

Mav didn't hesitate. He was all motion—shoulder, fist, fury. Craig swung, wild and messy. Mav ducked and landed a clean one to the jaw, then another. The refs moved but not fast enough. It took Zane and Kieran to pull them apart, dragging Mav back, his chest heaving and knuckles split.

Craig was still grinning. But it didn't reach his eyes.

"Well, that escalated." Selene crossed her legs and arched a brow.

That was when I saw the coaches. Their silence said everything. The look they gave Craig—that was new.

Both players were called off the ice and sent to the box. They would receive fines, maybe even a suspension. What had just happened couldn't go unpunished.

I was sick to my stomach and worried about Mav. After the game, the buzz hadn't died down. If anything, the tension in the air had sharpened. With a hug goodbye to Vivi and Selene, I slipped away from the stands and headed toward the press room, the muted noise of reporters and shuffling feet guiding me down the corridor. The team was expected to speak, and I knew Mav would be there. I needed to see how he dealt with the blowback.

When I entered, the room was packed with reporters, cameras, and so much noise. I stood near the back, arms folded, heart still echoing with every second of that fight.

It didn't take long for the coaches and several players to enter. As questions were fired, I gnawed on a fingernail, shifting from foot to foot. Mav answered with his usual calm, steering everything back to the team—always measured and focused.

Then they turned to Craig.

"There's been tension all season. Anything you want to clear up?"

Craig leaned into the mic. "Hockey's a physical sport. That's all it was."

But they kept pressing. "Your fiancée is Trina McNealy, Nyx Lawson's stepsister. Does that dynamic affect what happened tonight on the ice?" The silence that followed was heavy.

Craig smiled, but it was thinner now. "I'm here to play hockey. Family drama isn't my concern."

Then came the real blow. "We learned about Vince Lawson's will. Cynthia Lawson's financial decisions—cutting off her late husband's biological daughter while continuing to support her own. Does that sound like fair treatment to you?"

I felt faint, exposed. *How had they found out?* Then I remembered the woman with her phone pointed our way as our scene at the gala played out.

Craig's mask cracked. "No comment," he said tightly before pushing back from the table and standing to walk out.

"You don't get to walk away after that," Mav called, rising from his chair.

Craig turned around, jaw locked. "You don't get to act like you're the victim here."

Mav stepped toward him, the mic catching every word. "What the hell is your problem with me, Craig?"

"My problem is you don't belong here."

The room fell to a hush. Cameras pivoted. Mics leaned in.

Craig's voice sharpened. "You think just because you got a few goals and married the first groupie to smile at you in Vegas, you're some kind of star player?"

The reporters gasped.

"Enough," Harper muttered off-mic, but neither stopped.

"You hit me. You went after me on the ice," Mav said, his voice low and dangerous. "Own it."

Craig sneered. "You're a rookie who got lucky. And I wasn't going to sit back while you stole my spot. While you dragged this team into a tabloid scandal. After Jennings, they weren't going to let another rookie screw the franchise over," he spat. "Especially not one reckless enough to marry the first girl he met in Vegas."

"You mean the scandal you tried to start?" Mav snapped. "Because you couldn't handle the fact that someone younger, better, and not obsessed with covering his ass was coming up behind you?"

Craig took a step forward. "You have no idea what you've done."

"No," Mav shot back. "I know exactly what I've done. I've earned my place. You're the one who couldn't deal with the competition, so you came after me and the woman I love."

After the press conference, I waited in the hallway just outside the media room, my pulse still uneven, my thoughts spiraling. Mav found me there, his eyes scanning the corridor before they landed on me. Without a word, he stepped in close, his hand brushing mine.

"You good?" he asked, voice low.

I nodded, though I wasn't sure I meant it.

He leaned in, forehead almost touching mine. "It's going to be okay. They know who the real problem is now."

The tension that had been riding me since the game had started eased.

He squeezed my hand. "Wait for me in the lounge with Vivi and Selene. I just need five minutes with the coaches. Then we'll go home."

I nodded again, this time with more weight behind it. I watched him disappear through the locker-room doors before heading toward the lounge. All I wanted to do was head home and spend the rest of the night in his arms.

I slipped out early the next morning, leaving Mav in the shower and scribbling a note on the counter—just a quick coffee run. Decaf for me, of course. I needed fresh air and a few minutes of quiet, which didn't involve headlines or hushed voices.

The bell above the coffee-shop door jingled as I stepped inside. The place was mostly empty, save for a barista restocking pastries and a man in a suit hunched over his laptop near the window. The air smelled like espresso and cinnamon.

While I waited for our drinks, my phone buzzed. Vivi sent screenshots. Craig's name was plastered across every headline: trade speculation, locker-room conflict, PR crisis—the whole deal.

I read through one of the articles, waiting for the barista to call my name as two women entered and placed their orders. When my order was up, I curled my fingers around the paper cups and returned to the crisp morning air. I'd thought I could escape the drama for a moment, but the truth was it was a shitstorm. The one good thing was that, for once, it wasn't backfiring on me but rather on the people who deserved it.

The windows were open at home, and the TV played a muted sports recap while Mav sat on the couch, icing his knuckles in silence. A breeze moved through the room, carrying the scent of fresh laundry and clean cotton.

"You okay?" I asked.

He looked at me, eyes darker than usual. "Yeah. Just glad it's finally over."

"Think he'll be traded?"

"It's already in the works."

I didn't need to ask where. I didn't care. I moved closer and reached for his hand. "Thank you," I whispered.

He frowned. "For what?"

"For choosing me. Loudly."

His hand tightened around mine. "I always will."

Within days, the engagement between Trina and Craig was over. It wasn't public knowledge yet, but the whispers carried. There was speculation that Craig had been benched indefinitely or that a trade was already locked. I believed it.

CHAPTER THIRTY-SIX

MAV

The puck dropped, and I snapped into motion—no hesitation, no second-guessing. Everything on and off the ice finally felt right.

We'd both been issued fines, and I'd gladly paid mine. Ellis got hit harder. All the digs and the leaks to the press that Coach found out about had sealed his fate. With Ellis suspended, the vibe around the team had shifted for the better. He wouldn't be back, and that improved the mood even more. Tonight, we were playing like it—quick passes, clean hits, fast recoveries. Every line clicked, and energy buzzed through each shift.

St. James grinned at me after a fast breakout. "You're in the zone, Davis."

I bumped his shoulder as we skated toward the bench. "Guess clearing deadweight has its perks."

The guys laughed, but no one pushed back, not even Ellis's former crew. Everyone knew who I meant. No one was pretending anymore.

Coach gave me a nod from behind the glass, the look that said *keep it up*. That used to mean everything to me. *Now?* It still mattered—but not the way it used to. Not like she did.

W hen I walked into the condo that night, Nyx was curled on the couch in one of my old hoodies she favored, a baby-name book propped open in her lap like it held state secrets. Her dark hair was still damp from a shower, her face fresh, and the room's soft light made everything feel warmer. I froze for a second, just looking at her.

She glanced up, brow arched. "You're staring. That a stroke symptom or just residual adrenaline?"

I dropped my gear bag near the door and kicked off my shoes. "Neither. Just wondering how I got this lucky." She'd stayed home from the game, since she hadn't felt well. Morning sickness had turned into evening nausea, and I'd insisted she rest.

Her expression softened. "We both know luck had nothing to do with it."

I crossed the room, dropped beside her, and tugged her legs across my lap. "You sure? Because I'm still convinced the universe purposefully shoved us into each other that night in Vegas."

Nyx smirked. "You think fate roofied us?"

I laughed. "I think fate got drunk, handed us a pen, and said, 'Here, sign something stupid.'"

Her laugh was real and unguarded, and it settled something in my chest. She wasn't holding back. Not from me.

She closed the book and set it aside. "How was the game?"

"We crushed it. It felt different without Ellis. Better."

Nyx nodded slowly. "I figured. Vivi said the whole locker room was lighter at the morning skate."

"It was." I brushed my thumb across her ankle. "And the best part?"

"Let me guess," she said. "You didn't punch anyone."

I leaned in and kissed her bare knee. "Nope. The best part was coming home to you."

Her eyes flicked to mine, steady and warm.

"I meant what I said," I told her. "I'm all in, Nyx. This—us—it feels right. Even if it started backward."

She smiled and nodded, fingers sliding into mine. "Then let's stop looking back. We're here now." Then she pressed her lips to my ear and whispered, "I love you too."

My entire body went still. Then, slowly, I smiled. Like I'd been waiting for her to catch up. I turned my head slightly and brushed my lips over her temple. "Took you long enough."

She laughed softly and rolled her eyes, but she didn't pull away. And neither did I.

We sat there for a while, no words needed, just breathing in the kind of peace I never thought I would earn. It turned out that, sometimes, the best things started with a mistake that couldn't be undone.

EPILOGUE

NYX

One Year Later

The California sun spilled through the windows, bathing the living room in warm golden light. The soft hum of ESPN played in the background, the commentators raving about the undefeated season the team was having and how Mav was proving to be one of the best young forwards in the league. His name was all over the highlights, clips of him weaving around defenders, scoring impossible goals, and setting up plays like a seasoned veteran.

But right now? The tiny, sleeping baby cradled against my chest was the only thing that mattered. Emmett. He was barely three months old, a perfect mix of Mav and me—dark hair like both of us, but those piercing blue eyes were all Mav, and they melted me. His tiny fingers curled around the fabric of my shirt, his breaths soft and steady against my skin.

Mav's footsteps were quiet as he entered the room, but I still felt him before I saw him. His presence was that strong.

"How are my two favorite people?" he murmured, kissing the top of my head before pressing another to Emmett's.

"Perfect," I whispered because, in this moment, I truly was.

Mav sat beside me, stretching his long legs to rest his feet on the coffee table. He smelled like the ice, fresh from practice, his body still warm from the shower he'd taken after. "He's growing so fast," he said, voice filled with awe.

I smiled, smoothing my fingers over our son's chubby little cheek. "Too fast."

Mav shifted, wrapping an arm around my shoulders and pulling me into him. His heartbeat was steady beneath my palm, solid. Just like him. "Mom called earlier," he murmured after a moment.

I looked up at him, catching the emotion in his expression. "How's she doing?"

His jaw flexed, but it wasn't with tension—it was relief. "She's good," he said, his voice lighter than I'd heard in a long time. "She finally put the house on the market."

I blinked in surprise. "She's doing it?"

He nodded. "She's ready. She said she's got no reason to stay there anymore. She wants to be close to us… to Emmett."

My throat tightened. "Mav…"

"I know," he murmured before pressing a kiss to my temple.

Even miles away, the ripple effects of everything we'd fought through still lingered. Cynthia had been exiled from her country club circle, Trina had disappeared from the headlines, and Craig had faded into hockey's rearview mirror, traded and forgotten. They were no longer part of our story.

Mav's dad had fought like hell to be here for his grandson. He wasn't supposed to make it. The doctors had all but told us to prepare for the worst months before Emmett was born. But he did. He held on, fought through every brutal round of chemo, and refused to give in to the cancer that had been trying to steal him away for years. And he'd made it.

He was there in that hospital room the first time Mav placed Emmett in his arms. I'd never seen a man more determined to live than in that moment. He held on for every second he could. Until his body couldn't anymore.

Mav's mom had been by his side through it all, and she didn't fall apart when the time came to say goodbye. Not in the way I'd feared she would. She'd been saying goodbye all along, through those traumatic months of chemo and uncertainty. She also had us and a future to look forward to.

And Mav had made damn sure she never had to worry about anything again. He'd paid off their house. He'd filled her bank account with enough money to live comfortably for the rest of her life. He'd told his mom to quit her job as soon as he'd signed with the Titans and to spend those final months making memories instead of worrying about bills. And she had. Now, she was ready to start fresh and be here with us.

I pressed my face against Mav's shoulder and breathed him in. "She's going to love it here."

"She already does," he said, voice thick with emotion.

I pulled back and studied his face. He looked lighter than I'd ever seen him. Not just because his NHL career was taking off, not because ESPN couldn't stop talking about him, or even because his team was the best in the league. I released a slow breath, running my fingers over Emmett's tiny back. "Are you happy?"

Mav didn't hesitate. He reached over and gently traced his knuckles along my jaw. "Nyx, I've never been happier."

A lump formed in my throat, but I pushed past it. "Even with the diaper changes?" I teased.

He let out a chuckle, shifting to rub Emmett's back. "Even with the diaper changes."

"Even with my crazy pregnancy cravings?"

"The hot sauce you insisted on carrying around with us and

putting on everything was questionable, but yeah, even with that."

I laughed softly, curling into him more.

Ever since my dad had died, I hadn't known what happiness looked like. I hadn't thought it was something I would ever truly have again. But now, I had a husband who loved me, a son who was the best thing we'd ever done, and a future that finally felt like mine. No more running. No more questioning. This was where I was meant to be. And I wouldn't change a damn thing.

Continue reading more of Isla's books with the Hidden Valley Elite or Fall Lake Ballers series.

Looking for your next book to read? Check out more books by Amy McKinley/Isla Vaughn here: https://store. amymckinleyauthor.com/pages/reading-order

If you enjoyed reading SHATTERED ICE as much as I did writing it, I hope you'll consider leaving a review.

ALSO BY ISLA VAUGHN

Hidden Valley Elite Series

Savage Start

Savage Lies

Savage Truth

Brutal Days

Brutal Nights

Cruel Start

Cruel Hate

Cruel Love

Wicked Games

Wicked Ends

Fall Lake Ballers

Quarterback Keeper

Pump Fake

Red Zone

Power Plays & Pucks

Shattered Ice

Pucking Power Plays *(coming soon)*

Blackwood Blades *(coming soon)*

Iced Out

Cross-Check

Sudden Death

Isla Vaughn also publishes under *USA Today* bestselling author Amy McKinley.

Mafia Elite

No Way Out

Blood Oath

Born in Darkness

Savage Secrets

Ruthless Heir

Collateral Damage

Rivals

Gray Ghost Novels (Former Navy SEALs)

Moments That Define Us

Broken Circle

Eye of the Storm

Beneath the Surface

Vantage Point

Covert Threat

Marked for Death

Deadly Isles Special Ops (Navy SEALs)

Twisted Secrets

Bound by Secrets

Forged by Secrets

Standalone Titles

Shattered Melody

Siren's Call: Cursed Seas

Fake Fiancé (A Second Chance Office Romance)

Moonlit Destination Series

Moonlit Whisper

Moonlit Kiss

Moonlit Mirage

Five Fates Series

Hidden

Taken

Bound by Blood Mafia Series *(coming soon)*

Hidde Enemy

Stolen Prize

Secret Pawn

Broken Vow

Buried Rival

Tarnished Crown

ACKNOWLEDGMENTS

Shattered Ice was one of those books that wouldn't let go—loud, relentless, and emotionally tangled in all the best (and most challenging) ways. I couldn't have brought it to life without some truly incredible people by my side.

To my family—thank you for letting me disappear into fictional worlds and for never flinching when I emerge with wild eyes and deadline panic. Your patience, encouragement, and unwavering love give me the space to create. I couldn't do this without you.

To my critique crew—you know who you are. You catch me when I spiral, hype me up when I second-guess, and always know how to push me just far enough to make the story sharper, deeper, better. Kristin Kisska, Emily Albright, Candace Irving, and Jessica Riley Miller—thank you for being in the trenches with me, again and again. Your time, creativity, and honest insight mean the world.

Audrey Anhalt—thank you for bringing Mav and Nyx to life with such precision and warmth. That illustrated cover captures *everything*, and I'm endlessly grateful for your vision.

TE Black Designs, thank you for taking that illustration and making magic out of it. You consistently turn my vague concepts into jaw-dropping covers, and I'm always in awe. And to Red Adept Editing—thank you for your keen eye, thoughtful edits, and dedication to making this book shine. Your polish brings the final pages to life.

To Colleen Noyes and the entire team at Itsy Bitsy Book Bits

—thank you for championing my work with so much heart and hustle. You help bridge the gap between stories and the readers who are waiting to fall in love with them.

To every reader who picked up this book—whether it's your first of mine or your thirtieth—thank you. Your messages, reviews, and support are what keep me going. Truly. If you're not already in my newsletter crew, come join the chaos—I'd love to have you there.

With all my heart—thank you.

ABOUT THE AUTHOR

Isla Vaughn is the author of the Hidden Valley Elite and Fall Lake Ballers series. Her romance books are full of complex characters, strong alpha males, and the fierce women who bring them to their knees. When not writing, she can be found daydreaming about owning a beach house, reading, or drinking too much coffee.

instagram.com/islavaughnauthor
facebook.com/author.IslaVaughn
tiktok.com/@islavaughnauthor
goodreads.com/islavaughn_author
bookbub.com/profile/isla-vaughn